NOT OUR KIND
OF
KILLING

Books by
Joseph L.S. Terrell

Harrison Weaver Mysteries

TIDE OF DARKNESS
OVERWASH OF EVIL
NOT OUR KIND OF KILLING

Jonathan Clayton Novels

THE OTHER SIDE OF SILENCE
LEARNING TO SLOW DANCE

Stand Alones

A TIME OF MUSIC, A TIME OF MAGIC

A NEUROTIC'S GUIDE TO SANE LIVING

NOT OUR KIND
OF
KILLING

A HARRISON WEAVER MYSTERY

JOSEPH L.S. TERRELL

BellaRosaBooks

BellaRosaBooks

NOT OUR KIND OF KILLING
ISBN 978-1-62268-039-9

Copyright © 2013 by Joseph L.S. Terrell

First Printed: June 2013

Library of Congress Control Number: 2013942413

Also available as e-book: ISBN 978-1-62268-040-5

Printed in the United States of America on acid-free paper.

Cover photograph by Craig Faris, www.craigfaris.com.
Author photograph by Veronica Moschetti

Book design by Bella Rosa Books

BellaRosaBooks and logo are trademarks of Bella Rosa Books

10   9   8   7   6   5   4   3   2

With my love, this book is for Veronica,
who brings zest and joy into being.

Acknowledgments

My thanks to former FBI agent and friend Larry Likart for his guidance concerning serial killers and drugs that may be used; to always helpful manuscript readers Veronica Moschetti and Penny Thomas for their excellent and insightful editorial suggestions; and to authors Maggie Toussaint and Beth Terrell for their separate critiques, which certainly improved the story, and the writing; and especially to my editor and publisher, Rod Hunter of Bella Rosa Books, for having faith in me as a writer.

Author's Note:

I've chosen to compress time to use the historic courthouse in Manteo to house the sheriff's and other offices as it did in the past. While the main characters in this story are figments of my imagination, and do not represent real people either living or dead, they are quite real to me as I've lived with them for months and even years as I write about them. Some towns-people will recognize mention by name of a few actual persons, who know that I'm using their names. Also, most of the places written about actually exist. But the story, after all, is a made up story, for that's what fiction is all about. I hope you enjoy the tale.

–JLST

Chapter One

Buffalo City, tucked away two dusty miles off US 64 on the mainland in Dare County, used to be known as the moonshine capital of North Carolina.

Then it became a great place to launch a kayak into the Alligator River.

Or a place to dump a body.

A young female body.

Nude.

Hogtied

Shortly after dawn on that Saturday morning in May, I drove to Buffalo City to explore the backwaters in my kayak. I had pulled my Subaru Outback to the end of the dirt road, kayak affixed on top, and parked at the side of the little turnaround. From there I could ease the kayak into the shallow waters at the edge of the river.

I had just released the last strap so I could drag my kayak a short distance for launching, when I suddenly sucked in my breath: not ten yards away, a woman's bare legs protruded from the brush at the edge of the water. The legs were attached to a body partially obscured by low, dusty vegetation. My heart picked up beats, and I dropped the cord. Taking quick, shallow breaths, I glanced around, warily. Whether I actually expected to see someone else, I don't know. Maybe I thought I might be pounced upon at any moment. Everything was silent, except for a bird chirping happily in a pine tree. This had to be a dream, but if it was, it was a bad one.

I took a few unsteady steps toward the body.

I got closer, confirming it was a woman and she was nude. Her wrists and ankles were tied and there was a loop of rope around her neck that led back to her ankles. Her back was arched. Hogtied. A person could stay alive as long as they could keep their back arched. When fatigue took over, the person strangled from the noose. A tortuous way to kill someone. It would take a sadistic sonofabitch to do this, and to a pretty young woman.

She looked to be in her twenties, with light brown hair, a trim body. There was a small tattoo of an angel on her left ankle. An angel. To look after her, watch over her. Sure, hell yes.

It was not that warm, but I felt the beginnings of perspiration running down my sides. I tried deliberately to slow my breathing.

Standing there by the body, I flipped open my cell phone and punched in the sheriff's office in Manteo, a number I knew by heart. I realized I was trembling.

The dispatcher at the sheriff's office answered on the first ring and identified himself. I didn't recognize his name. I told him who I was and that I had found the body of a young woman at the kayak launching area in Buffalo City.

"Is she dead?"

"Yes," I said. "It's a body. The nude body of a young woman."

"Do you suspect foul play?"

"She's been hogtied, deputy."

"Give me your name again, and hold a minute."

When he came back on a few seconds later, he said that Deputy Dorsey was over in East Lake serving papers and he would be on the scene in just a few minutes."

"And sir?"

"Yes?"

"Don't leave the area."

"I won't."

I moved mechanically back a few steps, turned and walked with jerky steps to my car. Leaning against the front fender, forcing myself to take even breaths, I stared toward the woman's body. From this point, her body was not that visible. In the sand and gravel parking area between the body and me, the only footprints were those of mine when I'd walked to the launching area and saw the body, and then my returning footprints to the car. The ground appeared to have been swept clean of any other markings. Maybe the night breeze had done that. Perspiration ran down my chest underneath my loose-fitting T-shirt. I had on somewhat ragged khaki shorts and sandals.

My name is Harrison Weaver, a crime writer, and I live on the Outer Banks, those thin barrier islands along the coast of North Carolina, only thirty-some miles from here. And as a crime writer, I've seen my share of dead bodies, but never one I could literally have almost stepped on. And what made this discovery even more eerie is that it was so similar to an unsolved case I'd been assigned to write about a month earlier up in the mountains of North Carolina at a place called Bloody Mattaskeet County. A young woman was found nude and hogtied in the back seat of her car.

Four hundred miles away and there's another beautiful nude woman, done in the same way.

Slowly, and trying to step in mostly my same footprints, I made my way back toward the woman's body. Maybe partly out of curiosity and partly because it was my training, I knew I needed to take a closer look at her while I waited for Deputy Dorsey. Too, in the first sighting of her up close there was something about her facial features that struck me as odd. Bending over from the waist and being careful not to contaminate the crime scene, I peered at the woman's face. The noose was around her neck, but her face didn't look as if she had been strangled. The characteristics apparent when someone has been strangled—swollen, protruding tongue; bugged-out almost exploded eyes; deep impression into her throat from the rope—were not visible. She looked strangely peaceful. Her face was not distorted. I didn't see any obvious wounds on her body, and no bruises. Her lips were slightly parted; her eyes open only a slit. I didn't touch her, but no visible decomposition had begun. She couldn't have been there long. A fly landed on her lower lip, and I waved the fly away. There were other insects that had begun to climb along her bare feet. I wanted to shoo them away as well, but I knew that was futile. She wasn't feeling anything, ever again. Studying her face, I realized there was something vaguely familiar about her appearance. Had I ever seen her before? I couldn't be sure. Death, whether from natural causes or murder, does subtly—and sometimes not so subtly—change a person's appearance. She was definitely not someone I knew, but something familiar about her nagged at me.

My mind flashed back to the picture of the body I had seen of the victim in Mattaskeet County. The woman looked much the same, almost like she was posed—and not strangled. One of the few observant things the sheriff there had said was that it appeared she *may* have been killed before she was tied up.

I heard the sound of an approaching vehicle. A cloud of white dust from the sand and gravel road became visible before I could actually see the car.

I didn't think Deputy Dorsey could have arrived that fast. I backtracked to my Subaru. Then the car came into view. It was not the sheriff's deputy. It was a Dodge SUV with two kayaks strapped to the roof, and Maryland license tags. A man and woman pulled their Dodge up a short distance from my car, the dust still hanging in the air from their approach. I turned my head away from the mushrooming white dust and coughed once. The sun was getting warmer and the humidity rising. I could smell the dust, mixed with the scent of the warmed pine trees.

Getting out of their Dodge, the couple waved hands in greeting. I walked toward them.

"I'm afraid there'll be no kayaking this morning."

The man's smile vanished and his face took on a mixture of disappointment overridden with aggressiveness. "Yeah? And why not?" A muscular, fit man, he was dressed in what looked like brand new Spandex bicycle-type shorts and a tank top. Both of them appeared to be in their early thirties. She was dressed much the same as the man, only her braless tank top was more amply filled out.

"This has become a crime scene," I said. "There's a woman's body over there." I inclined my head in the direction of the launching area.

They stared in that direction. He started to say, "I don't—"

I heard the woman's sharp intake of breath. "Oh my God . . ." She shrank against their SUV. "There," she said, nodding toward the launch area. Automatically, I glanced over my shoulder. From where we stood, only the woman's bare lower legs were visible.

The man stepped back from me. "Who are you?" he said. "Are you a cop?" The aggressiveness was gone from his voice, replaced by maybe just a touch of fear.

"No," I said. "I came here to go kayaking, too. I walked up on the body. I've called the sheriff's office. A deputy is on his way . . . and more officers, too, I'm sure, very shortly."

He watched my face. "All right if we stay here?"

She said, "Oh, I don't know, Brad . . ."

"Sure you can stay," I said. "But there'll be a lot of activity shortly and you'll want to stay out of the way."

I could tell he mulled something over in his mind before he spoke. "You said a 'crime scene.' Does that mean, you know, that it's not natural causes?" He hesitated a moment, apparently weighing his thoughts carefully. "I mean, how do you know?"

"She's tied up. Nude." I couldn't help but add, well with maybe a tad of unjustified and rather juvenile sarcasm, "Makes you think right off that it's not from natural causes."

Then we heard the piercing wail of a siren. I saw another

dust cloud rising beyond the pine and live oak trees before I saw a Dare County sheriff's department cruiser coming up on us hell-bent-for-leather. The cruiser stopped abruptly, the plume of white dust roiling back on it and on to us. I covered my nose and eyes with my hands. Deputy Dorsey got out of the cruiser and met me halfway between his car and the Maryland SUV. He has blondish red hair, close cropped, and is edging toward being portly. I've known him for almost a year.

"What's going on, Mr. Weaver?"

I pointed toward the body, and told him what I had discovered when I arrived.

"Who are those people?" he asked, nodding toward the couple standing close to each other beside their SUV.

"They came up a short while ago, right after I called the sheriff's office, to go kayaking. They haven't approached the body. I'm the only one who has—I mean since she was deposited here."

Dorsey nodded. "Let's take a look."

We used my footprints again to get close to the body. Dorsey leaned forward to get a look. His face was drawn and much of the color appeared to have vanished from his usual ruddy complexion. "Jesus," he whispered. He puffed out a long sigh of breath. "I'm calling it in. Get more help. Better get rescue folks out here, too."

"The coroner and a hearse, you mean," I said softly.

"Yeah." He looked around. "I've got a roll of crime scene tape in the vehicle. Help me string it around?"

"Sure." Then I said, "We'll probably have some more kayakers arriving soon and we want to keep them away."

He swallowed audibly, took another quick look at the body and we retraced our steps back to his cruiser. I don't know, but I figured this was probably the first time young Deputy Dorsey had come up on a murder scene.

Watching Dorsey's reaction to seeing the body brought an abrupt realization to me about my own attitude. What was it? Had I become hardened to death and murder? Although

I'd never *discovered* a body before, as I did this morning, I had years ago been one of two of us who were the first ones on a scene where two police officers had been slain. And I had written about death and mayhem extensively. But I didn't want to become hardened and uncaring. Perhaps it was a bit of rationalization on my part, but I attributed my momentary lack of real emotion to my instincts of what needed to be done, and done quickly—notifying the authorities and securing the area. Then for the first time since I'd come upon the body, I permitted myself to think about the victim as a *person*, whoever she was. A short time earlier, probably much less than twenty-four hours, she'd been vibrant and alive, with dreams and hopes. Now that was ended forever. I could imagine her as woman walking happily down the streets of Manteo or sunning on one of the nearby beaches, a woman I could have seen and spoken to, not a victim. Not just a body.

Dorsey had popped the trunk to his cruiser and handed me the roll of crime scene tape. I was back acting mechanically. Dorsey got on his radio, calling in. We'd have a slew of activity here shortly. I affixed one end of the crime scene tape to the railing of a footbridge that spanned the launching area, and picked up a broken limb to place in the cul-de-sac at the center of the semicircle, securing the tape to it; the end of the tape was tied to a low bush several yards from the body. So a good section of the area was roped off.

Just as we finished, another kayaker arrived. He had a double-seated kayak on a small trailer. A more mature couple, sun-tanned and looking healthy, got out of their Jeep, quizzical expressions on their faces.

I gave them a quick rundown while Dorsey went back to his radio. The couple carefully pulled their Jeep around in the cul-de-sac, avoiding the tape, and parked on the right side of the road in an area designated for vehicles with trailers. "I'm not sure how long we'll stay," the man said. "My wife, you know . . ."

I went back to speak to Dorsey, who had signed off on

his radio. He stood beside his cruiser, chewing his lower lip and rubbing the palms of his hands on his trouser legs. "Jesus," he said again. "What a way to do somebody."

I didn't say anything.

In just a few minutes, here came another sheriff's department cruiser; then a State Trooper; and another deputy. I heard a siren. It was a unit from Dare County rescue squad. The place was rapidly getting populated. A third Dare County sheriff's cruiser pulled up. It was Chief Deputy Odell Wright, a good friend who had recently been promoted to chief deputy. Another kayaker arrived, saw all of the activity. The driver spoke to one of the deputies and then turned around and left. Deputy Wright told the second deputy who had arrived to go back to US 64 and block off the road except for official vehicles.

Wright came over to speak to me. "You were the first one here?"

"Yeah . . . not counting whoever put the woman there."

He gave me one of his looks, like don't-get-smart. But then he shook his head and gave just a trace of a smile. Wright has a wicked sense of humor. He's black and he will, from time to time, point to his silver nametag that says O. Wright and tell a stranger that he is one of the original Wright Brothers. He may even add that his crazy brother is working on a flying machine.

Except for the State Trooper, Wright kept everyone away from the body. The wind had picked up a bit and blew some of the sand over my original tracks, but more were being made following the same path I had taken. Wright fanned a hand at the dust. "We need rain," he muttered. He went back to his cruiser and used his radio. I stood beside him. He signed off on the radio and turned to me. "Deputy Sellers will be here shortly with his camera. We need to record as much of this as we can." He wrinkled his brow, staring toward the place where the body lay. "Also, Dr. Willis." Willis was the acting coroner.

More to himself than to me, Wright said, "We're going

to need to get the state boys, SBI, involved in this."

"Yeah," I said. I figured that my friend SBI Agent T. (for Thomas) Ballsford Twiddy would undoubtedly get involved. This was his general area for investigations. He lived now near Elizabeth City.

Agent Twiddy, or Balls as all of his friends called him, knew that I had gone up to Bloody Mattaskeet on assignment to write about that unsolved murder. Thinking about that, and the similarity with this one, sent a fresh and chilling bit of perspiration running down my chest. I wasn't about to mention my thoughts to anyone other than Balls, even to Odell Wright. After all, the murders were four hundred miles apart.

Yet, I had that gut feeling—heck, more than just a gut feeling—that they were somehow linked. They had to be. Bizarre, I know. But this was too similar.

And I don't believe in coincidences—only messages that we may not understand at first, messages that have to be deciphered.

Chapter Two

Within an hour and a half of when I had discovered the body, Buffalo City appeared to have once again been populated. The name, Buffalo City, dates back to the turn of the Twentieth Century when it actually was a "city," the most populous area in the county, a thriving lumber camp with its own company store and currency. After the Upstate New York lumber company had harvested the trees, moonshining took over by some of the workers who remained there. Now, there's no sign that the area was ever populated—except by pine and live oak trees, scrubby vegetation and ferns, along with a goodly supply of wild critters, including black bears, river otters, red wolves, deer, and three varieties of poisonous snakes.

Another two official vehicles had arrived. The air crackled with radio chatter. I fully expected Sheriff Albright to arrive shortly. Maybe even my nemesis, officious District Attorney Rick Schweikert.

Acting Corner Willis, looking his usual rumpled self, wearing his not-quite tucked-in white shirt and tie, somewhat askew, had pulled up in his dusty Toyota, made even dustier by his ride to the area over the road into Buffalo City. He spoke to Odell Wright. Rescue squad members I knew, Pam and Duncan, joined them. Dr. Willis apparently told Pam and Duncan to hold off a while. Deputy Sellers stepped carefully around the woman's body, taking pictures from different angles.

The couple from Maryland came over and stood beside me as I leaned against the front fender of my Outback. He shook his head as if in disbelief. "I mean this is really something," he said. "Never expected something like this. Not here at the Outer Banks."

"We're not at the Outer Banks," the woman said. "We're miles from the beach . . . but you wanted to come here to kayak."

"Same area, more or less," he said, not looking at her but watching as Dr. Willis and Pam and Duncan approached the body.

The three were bent over at the waist, peering at the woman. Pam suddenly straightened up and said something to the other two. I couldn't hear what she said but her gestures and the obvious excitement in her manner told me that she may have recognized the woman. I was determined to speak privately to her later. Dr. Willis had donned latex gloves and I saw him reach a hand toward what had to be the woman's neck. Deputy Odell Wright approached them along the sandy path we had created. Dr. Willis turned to Wright and said something, inclining his head toward the woman.

I figured I knew what Dr. Willis said—that the woman wasn't killed by being hogtied, that she had been killed by some other method and *then* tied up.

In a few minutes, while I remained leaning against my car, Odell Wright walked somberly over to me. He had a notepad in his hand. "I'll need to get a statement from you." He gave me a weak smile, one tinged with a bit of sadness. "You know, like they do on TV. What time you got here, whether you saw anyone else here or leaving. The usual stuff."

I nodded. "Sure." I had seen Odell on his cell phone, so I asked, "Have you talked with Sheriff Albright yet?"

"Oh, yeah," he said. "Sure."

I couldn't tell whether he might have been offended by my question. "None of my business, I know. But I wondered if he wanted, you know, to come out before the body was moved. Maybe get some of the state guys to look over the situation."

There was a definite glare at me for a moment. Then Odell relaxed his shoulders. "Nope. He said just document the scene, the body." He shook his head a bit. "Said he was depending on me."

"And well he should," I said.

"Yeah, thanks. Thanks a lot."

"I'm serious."

"This is new to me, Weav. Not sure how much I like it." He held the notepad up, pen poised. He was ready to talk to me. Then he inclined his head toward the Spandex-clad Maryland couple. "Better talk to them, too. They came up right after you, didn't they? See if they saw anything you didn't."

After I'd chatted a minute or two with Odell, and he took notes in the small spiral notebook, he strolled over to the Maryland couple, notebook at the ready. Every few moments I saw the woman shake her head and shrug. I knew Odell was not coming up with anything useful, but he was covering the bases, as he should and as I knew he would.

Odell finished with the couple. Dr. Willis motioned to Odell to join him at the body. EMTs Pam and Duncan stood patiently nearby. Dr. Willis talked to Odell a few minutes. Odell nodded, looked at his watch and jotted down the time. Then Dr. Willis apparently gave the word to Pam and Duncan. They went back to the emergency vehicle and removed a gurney with collapsible legs. There was a brown rubberized body bag on the gurney.

Dr. Willis carefully tried to untie the rope that kept the woman's body arched. He finally ended up, though, cutting the rope about midway. The woman's body unbent slightly. Deputy Sellers took more pictures of the body as they began to move it, turning her over. Pam and Duncan, with Dr. Willis's help, had a difficult time getting the woman's body mostly into the body bag. They had trouble with her legs.

They left the rope ends attached to her.

The woman from Maryland turned away from the scene. She spoke loud enough for me to hear her say to the man, "I don't want to stay here. Let's go. Now!" Then she added, "Please." She got into their SUV. He went over to Odell and gave him a business card he had retrieved from his vehicle. He jotted something on the back of the card. The man glanced once more at the activity with the body, then turned and walked with slightly wobbly steps to his SUV. He started the engine and sat there for a few moments before turning slowly in the cul-de-sac and driving away. She stared straight ahead.

The humidity had definitely risen. I felt slightly nauseated. I got a bottle of water from my Subaru and took three big swallows.

Odell watched Duncan and Pam load the gurney into the emergency vehicle. Looking down at the ground, he stood there a moment. I took a couple of deep breaths and walked slowly over to Odell.

He glanced up at me. Almost to himself he said, "They're going to get the body over to Chapel Hill. Let the M.E. do an autopsy." Almost as if he was questioning himself, he said, "I guess that's the next step."

"What about ID-ing her, Odell?" I said. "Notifying . . . someone?"

"Yeah, that too." He seemed weighted down. He turned and watched as Duncan closed the rear doors to the emergency vehicle. "Pam thinks she knows who the woman is. Or at least thinks she's seen her, knows where she was working."

"That's a start," I said.

Odell nodded. We watched the emergency vehicle pull slowly away, maneuvering carefully around the Dare County Sheriff's Department cruisers. Odell said, "You know, Weav . . ." He shook his head. "I'll be glad to turn this over to the state guys. Agent Twiddy or somebody."

After securing my kayak on the roof of my car, I prepared to leave. Odell had assigned one of the deputies to stay on the scene. Wasn't sure how long he was supposed to stay, or what he was supposed to do. Figured it wasn't any of my business. Not really. I drove back up the road toward US 64, keeping my speed not much above a crawl in a vain effort to keep the dust down as much as possible. Not much luck with that, however. Yes, we really did need some rain.

At the highway, the deputy stationed there studied me a moment, then waved me on. I turned right and headed toward Mann's Harbor and the bridge over Croatan Sound to Manteo. I kept going toward Nags Head and the beaches. At Whalebone Junction, I swung north on 158, a four-lane highway with a left-turn lane in the middle. It is called the Bypass, but it doesn't bypass anything. It runs north and south along the Outer Banks, with businesses and stores on both sides lined up along its length. Traffic was fairly light because it was still early in the season. Just beyond the Dare Centre in Kill Devil Hills, I turned left into my development. I live in a little two-bedroom house on the sound side of 158. I've been there two years now. Blue house back in a cul-de-sac, somewhat secluded. I love it.

I parked my car in the carport and struggled a bit getting the kayak off and stowed between the utility room and my eighteen-foot Ranger outboard. So much for kayaking today. I went up the stairs on the outside of the house and into the kitchen and dining area where I do my writing at a table I have set up at the two windows, facing south. As soon as I walked in, Janey, my parakeet, began chirping and doing her head-bopping dance. She likes company. I've had her for three years now and although female parakeets are not supposed to talk, she's picked up two words—not very nice words—that I've apparently muttered repeatedly while prac-ticing my upright bass fiddle. Although I have a stand for it, the bass is almost always lying on its side in the middle of the small living room.

I spoke to Janey and gave her a sprig of millet seeds. I stepped over the neck of the bass and went to the phone.

There were two calls I needed to make, but first I checked for messages. Yep, there was one. I punched in the play button and listened to the snide, nasal voice of District Attorney Rick Schweikert:

"Well, Mr. Weaver, I see you've once again managed to get yourself involved in a heinous crime. Oh, I know you'll say you're not involved, but after all, you were the one who just *happened* to discover a body."

I knew that Chief Deputy Wright had spoken with Sheriff Albright, who in turn surely filled in Schweikert on the events of the morning.

Schweikert continued. "So, if it's not too much trouble for you, Mr. Weaver, I'd like to have a chat with you, say, Monday morning about ten o'clock. I'd be fascinated to hear your account of discovering the body."

He signed off. I sat there a moment thinking about Schweikert, that neo-Nazi son of a bitch. He can't abide me, nor I him, and it all dated back to a magazine piece I'd written in which I described him as the smug bastard he is.

I tried to put him out of my mind. I knew I'd see him Monday morning, and probably along with Sheriff Albright, a kindly man whom I liked. It might even be a meeting that included Deputy Wright—and perhaps my friend, SBI Agent Twiddy.

Ballsford Twiddy was one of the two people I needed to call. I punched in his cell number. I got his voice mail. "Balls," I said, "you've probably already heard about the woman whose body I found in Dare County this morning— Buffalo City—hogtied. I'm sure you'll get involved in the investigation. I haven't mentioned the similarity of this one today to that piece I started to work on in the mountains last month. So I'd like to talk with you a bit—maybe break-fast?—Monday morning before I meet with my dear friend Rick Schweikert. Give me a ring back this weekend if you can."

Now I needed to call Elly. Her name is Ellen Pedersen but everyone calls her Elly. Okay, yes, we're getting closer all the time. Elly is a young widow—a mere thirty-one—with a five-year-old son, Martin, who has finally gotten so he will speak to me, most of the time. I'm a bit older than Elly. All right, a good nine and a half years older.

I took the phone's handset out on the porch with a reheated cup of coffee I'd made early that morning. I knew it wouldn't be fit to drink, but it gave me something else to think about as I sipped on it. In my mind, I composed what I would say to Elly. I took a breath and keyed in her number.

Her phone was picked up before the first ring completed. There was a fumbling sound as if someone almost dropped the phone. Then a tiny voice said, "Yes?"

Not Elly, certainly, and I thought I recognized the voice. "Lauren, is that you?" She's a four-year-old who lives next door to the house Elly, Martin, and Elly's mother share in Manteo. Lauren spends a lot of time at the Pedersen's and she loves to answer the phone.

The tiny voice again: "Yes."

"Is Elly there, Lauren?"

"Yes." A long pause with only silence.

"Would you please get her on the phone?"

"Yes." Nothing. No movement that I could hear.

Here we go again, I thought. Lauren is good at answering the phone but pretty dismal with follow-up. But then I heard Elly in the background say, "Thank you, Lauren. I'll take the phone now." There was still a light-hearted lilt to her voice when Elly came on the phone.

"This is Harrison," I said. Elly is one of the few people who calls me by my first name, and she does it with her soft "hoigh-toide" fast-disappearing Outer Banks accent.

But the light-heartedness in her voice disappeared, replaced by a tone of concern. "Mabel called me this morning and told me what you found at Buffalo City." Mabel has worked for many years at the sheriff's department and Elly works in the same building in the Register of Deeds office. "It looks like you just can't stay away from getting involved in . . . in this sort of thing."

"Well, I certainly wasn't trying to get involved. Just go kayaking."

"Harrison, you may not try to get involved but—but, you've got a talent for it, if *talent* is the word to use." Then she held the phone away from her face. "You two go on outside and play." She came back to me. "Sorry. Martin and Lauren were right under foot." She sighed audibly. "Can you promise me—*promise* me—that you won't get involved in this one? Not again . . ."

"Well, Elly, I'm not really involved. I just happened to come upon the body. That's all."

"You're involved."

"Maybe just tangentially."

"Tangentially? You're always only involved tangentially . . . to start with." I heard her puff out a breath of air. "*Tangentially*! That's a lot of hooey."

"I didn't know anyone ever said hooey. Not in this century."

"I've got some other choice words I could use, but the children are just outside." Her voice had become tinged with a touch of humor. I could imagine a slow smile beginning to edge along her lips. Nice lips, too.

"I still wish you would become a romance writer, instead of true-crime," she said.

"I like romance," I said. "And speaking of romance . . . May I come over tonight after supper?"

"Yeah, yeah," she chuckled. There was a pause and then her voice got serious again. "I know what kind of story you went to the mountains to do. And I know how that poor woman was killed. Now this one at Buffalo City. But . . ."

"Have you mentioned that to anyone?"

"No. I thought about it as soon as Mabel told me about this one. I almost blurted out something about the . . . the you know, hogtieing. But I didn't."

"Good."

"I knew you wouldn't want me to."

I told her about Schweikert wanting to talk to me Monday morning. I told her, too, that I was hoping to talk with Agent Twiddy before meeting with Schweikert.

"I hope so, too," she said. "You know Schweikert will be all questioning you on this, trying to make you out as a suspect or something if he can."

"I know."

There was a pause again on her line while apparently she mulled something over. "Harrison?"

"Yes?"

"You didn't know this woman at Buffalo City, did you?"

Chapter Three

There was a momentary flash of—what? irritation?—at Elly's question as to whether I knew the victim. But just as suddenly as the feeling surfaced, it disappeared. I knew she was asking a very logical question. She was not playing games or casting any suspicion. She didn't play games. So before we signed off, I told Elly that, no, I didn't know the woman; I did add that there was something familiar about her, as if maybe I had seen her somewhere around the Outer Banks. I didn't tell her, however, that I felt that EMT Pam recognized her. I didn't know that for certain. Just as well until we got a positive ID. What did I mean by "we"? This wasn't my investigation. I know, I know. I have a hard time not getting involved, just like Elly said.

I really wanted to talk with Balls, to give him details of what I ran into up at Bloody Mattaskeet—and that similar murder, the one I kissed off because it was botched so haphazardly that I didn't even want to write about it.

Also, I needed to call Rose Mantelli, my editor who had me go up to Bloody Mattaskeet. This latest murder put a whole different slant on whether there was a story or not. I decided to call her Monday morning when I returned from my meeting with Schweikert.

That evening after an early light supper at my house, I drove over to Manteo to see Elly. Just as dusk was coming on, I pulled up in the graveled driveway to her rather secluded street on a side road near the Manteo airport. She came out onto the front porch and wiggled her raised fingers to me in greeting, as I knew she would. I gave her a discreet hug, and we went inside. On the end table under a lamp by the sofa, a section of newspaper was folded to the crossword puzzle.

"Get it done?" I asked, nodding toward the crossword.

"Just about. Saturday's is always the hardest, more so than Sunday." She is avid about crossword puzzles and usually has one with her, in her purse or beside her desk at the Register of Deeds office that she sneaks a look at as soon as there's a lull in the moment's activity. In addition to crosswords, she's addicted to ancient history and will launch into tales about the Punic Wars or the fall of Carthage with only a bit of prompting. She especially takes pleasure in regaling her friend Linda Shackleford of *The Coastland Times* with bits of history, just to watch Linda give one of her exasperated audible sighs, complete with facial expressions that would have made Harpo Marx envious.

Elly wore trim off-white cotton slacks and sandals and a peach-colored golf shirt. Her dark hair was pulled back and secured with some sort of clasp that women wear. I liked the way one or two of her hairs escaped the clasp and brushed against her slender neck. Like many of the natives here at the Outer Banks, she managed to avoid the sun. Her skin remained fair and unblemished except for a small strawberry-colored birthmark on her throat just below the right jaw line.

We stood there in the small living room, a grin pasted on my face. I could smell the pleasant odor of Mrs. Pedersen's cooking. I liked the home feeling it gave me. "You look nice," I said, and added, ". . . as always."

"Thanks." Then, "It's nice outside," she said. "Want to sit on the porch?"

We sat on the porch in the swing and talked. I kept trying to turn the conversation away from finding the woman's body at Buffalo City, and also trying vainly and probably untruthfully to convince Elly that I would not get involved in the investigation. There had been two other cases since I'd moved here—both of which I had become deeply involved with: one that put Elly in danger and another one that came close to getting me killed.

Dark had come on. At one point Elly had to excuse herself to go into the house to help her mother get Martin ready for bed. I sat there staring out toward the pine trees and thinking about my trip to Bloody Mattaskeet. There just had to be a connection and I kept going over details of my trip to the mountains, the people I'd met. The experience there wasn't pleasant. I knew I'd go over it in detail with Agent Twiddy, but for now I came up with nothing.

A short time later Elly marched a reluctant Martin out to say goodnight to me. He had on faded blue cotton pajamas that were getting a bit short for him in the legs.

Martin mumbled something to me, which I assumed was telling me goodnight, all the while staring at the floor and holding to his mother's leg.

"Martin, do you want to give Mr. Harrison a hug goodnight?"

"No," he said, and clung more tightly to his mother's leg. But then he turned his face toward mine; a smile played shyly about his lips, like maybe he didn't really mean the "no."

The two of them went inside.

I knew that when she returned after getting Martin settled in, she'd want to talk further about the murdered girl.

She sighed softly when she came back and sat beside me on the swing. "Mother's reading him a story." She stared off toward the huge live oak tree that dominated part of the front yard. Large, low branches hung down, making something of a canopy under which Martin and his little friend Lauren played. Elly pursed her lips. "I probably should be the one reading him the story . . ."

"Do you need for me to go, let you get back in there?"

"No. No, Mother can handle it tonight. Thank goodness for her."

Mrs. Pedersen was taller than Elly, sturdier in appearance, with her short, steel-gray hair, erect bearing. From family pictures I had seen, I knew that Elly more strongly resembled her father, a displaced native of Minnesota who had come to the area with the Coast Guard, met the future Mrs. Pedersen, and stayed here the rest of his life, which ended at least ten years ago. Even when she was married, Elly kept her maiden name of Pedersen.

Elly turned toward me. "Okay, Harrison, what's the connection between the killing up in the mountains and this one today?"

"Well, I don't know that there is any connection." It's true; I didn't know *positively* that there was a connection.

"Aw, come on now. You know it's going to come out. Rick Schweikert is going to find out—if he doesn't already know—that you went up to that place in the mountains, Bloody Mattaskeet or whatever it's called, and looked into a murder just like this one." She put her hand on my arm. "Then he's going to be all over you, all over again."

"Yeah, he does like to hassle me. I know that."

"He thinks you attract dead bodies like a magnet. Murder seems to follow you around."

"Heck, Elly, I'm a crime writer. Of course there's . . . well, bodies do show up. But usually I don't stumble on them like I did this morning." We were quiet for a minute or so, both staring off toward the trees. I was thinking I needed to be more straightforward with Elly. So I broke the silence. "To tell you the truth, I've been thinking the same thing you're thinking—that there may very well be a connection between the two killings. I mean, how bizarre would it be to have two women hogtied four hundred miles apart. But I have no idea—not the slightest inkling—what the connection could possibly be . . ." I gave a short chuckle. ". . . unless, of course, the obvious: the same killer." I didn't tell Elly that I believed, just from viewing the woman at Buffalo City, that she was not strangled with the rope but was already dead when she was trussed up, or that the sheriff in Bloody Mattaskeet intimated he thought the same thing about the woman there.

Suddenly Elly stood. It was a dismissive stance, and directed toward me. "That's all we ever talk about, it seems—murder and killing and . . . and, I don't know . . ."

I stood and took her hand. I didn't know what to say, but I mumbled something about that's not all we talk about, surely. It was dark there on the porch and I hugged her close to me. She felt tense and resisting at first. Then her body began to relax and felt softer—for a moment. She pulled slightly away from me so she could look into my eyes. "It really gets depressing at times. I can't help it. It does."

I nodded.

"We'll try to talk less about it," I said.

She gave a sad little smile. "Sure," she said, stretching the word out.

"Really. We can talk less about it."

"I'd better go in. Mother wants to leave early in the morning to see Aunt Sarah. Spend the day in Greenville."

"Okay," I said. We kissed goodnight, but it was more perfunctory than passionate.

As I drove back toward my house, I was depressed. Not much of a date. I knew Elly felt much the same way. From time to time she did pull back, put an invisible shield between us. We had been seeing each other for close to two years now, and just when I thought it was progressing to what people call "the next level," something happened and put a damper on things. Mostly her feelings, I really believed. I *think* I'm ready for our relationship to move forward. Honestly, though, sometimes I guess I have mixed feelings also. I'm sure that my reluctance for full commitment is because, like Elly, I had lost my spouse also. My wife, Keely, died two and a half years ago. I still have a difficult time saying it, but she committed suicide. Pills. She was a vocalist with several bands, some of which I played with; she had a beautiful, alto voice, a lot like Adele. But depression began to envelope her. No way I, or anyone else, could reach her. I still don't understand suicide. It saddens me to think of her final months, and then finding her curled up in the bed. Dead. I can remember with a shudder putting my hand on her shoulder when I found her and it was like touching something as immovable and unyielding as a bag of cold sand.

Yes, I carry baggage. I guess we all do. Elly has that also, plus I know her feelings have something to do with my involvement in writing about crime—and getting involved in investigations—but that's not all of it. She was hurt terribly when her young husband, who was sickly in the beginning, came down with an especially virulent flu-type virus and died. He wasn't even thirty. Since then she has steeled herself against losing her heart again.

I concentrated on driving when I realized I'd almost run through a red light at Whalebone Junction. Traffic was beginning to pick up. Wouldn't be long now before the roads were clogged with cars, the majority of which would carry license plates from Virginia, Pennsylvania, New Jersey, Ohio, and tags other than North Carolina.

I'd left a lamp on in my house so that it would look homey when I returned. Now the light streamed through the front window and out over the bird feeders on the outside railing. The birds made a mess with the seeds and hulls, but I enjoyed feeding them.

I stood outside for a minute or two, looking at the stars and breathing in the night air. I always thought I could smell the ocean, a quarter of a mile away: a humid, slightly salty, female scent. When the traffic on the Bypass was light and the tide was high, I could actually hear the ocean's surf. It was very faint, but I could hear it, and sense its power.

When I went up the outside stairs and into the kitchen area, I could see the answering machine blinking on the table in the living room. It was Balls, as I thought it might be.

"Weav, I see you stepped in it again. No wonder Schweikert wants to talk to you." His voice was husky, authoritative, cop-tough when needed; but among friends a hint of amusement frequently seeped through in his tone. "Sure, we can have breakfast, talk. We'd better. Don't know whether Schweikert knows about your trip to Mattaskeet, but I suspect he does. Now this one." I heard Balls' wife, Lorraine, saying something in the background, probably to one of their two teenage children.

Balls continued: "Meet at Henry's at eight o'clock. You're buying." He chuckled. "Now don't bother me anymore until then. Okay? Going to church tomorrow with Lorraine. Hell, would do you some good to get to church, too. Help atone for some of those sins . . . sins you'd like to be committing at any rate."

Then he got serious. "I want to hear a lot more about your trip to Mattaskeet, who you met with, what they said, your impression of what was going on up there . . . because of this thing down here. Very strange, Weav. Very strange indeed."

After I shut the answering machine off, I stood there a moment. Janey began to chirp, trying to get my attention. Mechanically I moved over to her cage, put my hand inside the cage to let her nibble at my fingers. Time to cover her up, let her go to sleep. I retrieved her cage cover from where I keep it in one of the bookcases.

I moved like I was sleepwalking. Yes, I thought, very strange. Very strange indeed.

Chapter Four

I spent Sunday puttering around my little house. I practiced the bass for almost forty minutes. Janey loves the activity and the sound. I practiced with the bow primarily. Did a few pizzicato jazz riffs. She especially likes those. I watched my language when I tried more of the tough classical pieces. The expletives I muttered in trying to master a section of Mozart's Requiem a year or so ago became the only two words Janey could mimic. She says those two words with great clarity.

After practicing, I went out on the deck with a cup of coffee. Since the weather was in the high seventies and not much wind, I brought Janey's cage out on the deck. She tries to get the attention of other birds, but they treat her with frank indifference. For a moment or two, the thought played around the edge of my mind of going to the beach and flailing the waters a bit with a surfcasting rod, see what might want to hit a piece of shrimp. But lethargy took over instead and I just sat there enjoying the weather, the blue sky with only a few puffy clouds moving slowly from the northwest, and looking out at the scrubby pine trees and the one wildly growing live oak in the vacant lot next door. I could smell the sun hitting the vegetation, and that made me think about Mattaskeet County when I arrived there and got out of my car, took a deep breath; the scent of fir and pines was so strong that it smelled like Christmas there in the spring.

Then, naturally, I started going over in my mind all that happened in Mattaskeet and what I could relate to Balls tomorrow morning, see if he could come up with any angles I had not thought of.

Late that afternoon I got to really missing Elly. It would be close to dark before she and Martin and her mother returned, and I wouldn't see her tonight. I replayed in my mind her mood from last evening, trying to think if there was some way to ease her concerns. Maybe time will make it easier for her and for me to relax and let life start again.

Janey chirped and made me come out of it. She was doing her head-bobbing dance, trying vainly to get the attention of a blue jay that had landed on the far end of the railing, partaking of the spilled seeds from the feeder. "Might as well forget it, Janey," I said. The jay cocked his head at me when I spoke, and then went back to the seeds.

Monday morning I was up early, showered and dressed in a reasonably pressed pair of khakis, golf shirt, and boat shoes with even a pair of socks. I stuck a narrow reporter's notepad in my back pocket, along with a good ballpoint pen. In talking with Balls, I wanted to make notes of anything that occurred to me concerning Mattaskeet and a possible connection with Buffalo City. Balls and I went back several years when I was a reporter with a daily newspaper and just starting in the crime writing business. I'd covered him on a couple of cases he was working on, and I was able to relay some information to him on one of the cases that helped him solve it. He appreciated it—and that I knew when to keep something off the record and keep my mouth shut. After that he said he considered me his "lucky charm," and had confided in me on cases, knowing that I would when necessary, indeed, keep my mouth shut and my pen in my pocket.

Driving back up a couple of miles to Henry's just before eight, I glanced at the blue sky. My windows in the Subaru were lowered. Another lovely spring day. Traffic had picked up a bit; a number of cars headed south, coming onto the islands from up around Currituck and going to various jobs. I paused in the middle turn lane, waiting for a break in the traffic, my blinker on. I turned left into Henry's parking area. Several cars had nosed into spaces. Immediately I saw Balls' souped-up Thunderbird—nose out near the front entrance. Always nose out so he can make a speedy departure if necessary. Henry's is a favorite breakfast place for many of the locals.

Inside I greeted Henry's pretty wife, Linda, whose smiling face is framed with medium-length prematurely gray hair. I nodded toward one of the booths in the back and said, "I'm meeting someone." She started to lead me back but I told her it wasn't necessary. She handed me a menu, the smile still there.

Balls sat there grinning. We shook hands as I took my seat opposite him. "Just can't help but flirt with the ladies, can you?" he said, tilting his head toward Linda.

"Just being friendly, Balls."

He looked good, still sporting his Tom Selleck mustache. He wore a light tan sports jacket and blue button-down oxford shirt. He even had on a maroon knit tie. The big grin remained. He had a half-empty cup of coffee. "Well, so once again you go for an inquisition before your friend Schweikert. Looks like you can't stay out of his gun sight." Balls took a noisy sip of his coffee.

"Yeah, you know how crazy he is about me."

"You do manage to get—what we'll call—involved," he said, the grin fading as he got serious.

I shrugged.

The waitress, a friendly red-headed young woman I'd seen at Henry's before, came to our table with two menus. She told us about the omelet specials as she placed the menus on the table. Balls ordered the three-egg crab-filled omelet, with a side order of bacon. I got the ham and cheese omelet and coffee. We both opted for toast rather than the biscuits. She brought me my coffee and refilled Balls'.

"Okay," he said, looking directly at my eyes, "let's talk about the victim you found at Buffalo City. And I want to know all about your trip to Mattaskeet County and what you learned there. I want to know everything you can remember about the trip up there."

"You'll be working this local case?"

"I'm already working it."

I should have known that. He'd probably been on the phone Saturday and yesterday talking with the deputies, the M.E., and others. "You think there's a connection?"

"What do you think, Sherlock?"

"You know I don't believe in coincidences."

"Yeah, yeah. I know. But sometimes, Weav, there are coincidences. This could be one. Maybe even a copycat."

In the few minutes it took for the omelets to arrive, I gave Balls a rundown of my trip to Buffalo City. He nodded several times as he listened. I sensed he knew it all anyway.

We thanked the waitress when she brought our food. She left us to go to an older couple two booths away. Balls was quiet a moment as he attacked his omelet. He picked up a piece of bacon in his fingers and took a bite to go with the omelet. Still chewing, he said, "The woman has been identified. Got a little background on her."

He hadn't wasted any time. I waited for him to say more, but he was silent, appearing to concentrate on eating. A ploy of his: He waited for me to say something.

"Balls, I'm no expert on viewing bodies, but I wondered about the hogtieing. It didn't look like she'd been . . ."

He stopped eating, stared at me, as I let my voice trail off. "What were you getting ready to say?" he asked.

"I just wonder if she was really killed by being hogtied. I mean, she looked sort of peaceful, not like she'd been strangled with that rope and struggled and all."

He didn't say anything for a moment, as if he weighed what he would reveal to me. Quietly he said, "She was already dead. Then tied up. That's the preliminary opinion of the M.E."

I nodded.

We were silent for a minute or so, each of us concentrating on our food and our private thoughts. Balls nodded toward the toast. "You going to eat any of that toast?"

I had taken a half a slice. I shook my head. "Not any more."

He took the remaining two halves and opened one of the little containers of grape jelly, slathering a section of toast and stuffed it in his mouth. He washed down the toast with a swig of his coffee. Then he looked at me with those cop eyes again: "Mattaskeet. What about the woman there?"

I shook my head, remembering how disgusted I felt about the so-called investigation. "I saw pictures of the body the sheriff showed me. She looked just like this woman, like she had been posed. She was hogtied, but . . ."

As I paused, Balls said, "Face not distorted, tongue swollen, eyes bugged out?"

I nodded again. "Even the sheriff mentioned he thought she'd been killed elsewhere, then tied up . . . but he let the family take her immediately. She wasn't from there, somewhere up north. Ohio. Cremated. No autopsy, nothing."

I signaled our waitress for a refill on the coffee. She refilled both of our mugs. She wore tight-fitting jeans and a white blouse. The top button had come undone or never buttoned. She smiled and asked if everything was all right. "Very good," I said.

Balls grinned at me when she went to refill coffee for the couple two booths away. "Just can't keep your eyes off the ladies, can you?"

"Hell, Balls. I was just being pleasant."

"Uh-huh. Sure. I saw you eyeing her."

I shook my head. "Okay, back to murder and mayhem."

Just like that he got serious again. "Okay," Balls said, "let's go over what it is you will tell Schweikert. Start with, we don't know how much he knows about your trip to Mattaskeet, what you saw there, what you learned." He moved his coffee mug away, toying with the handle. "But we've got to assume—knowing how this town is—that he knows you went up there and what the story is that you were supposed to be working on. Another victim hogtied, or at least tied up. Case unsolved."

"*Supposed* to be working on is right," I said. "I wasn't up there twelve hours before I knew that the investigation was so botched that the only way I could write it would be to make the sheriff and other lawmen look like incompetents . . . or worse." I looked across at Balls. "My editor wants to make the cops look good, not the other way around."

"I understand," Balls said. "Just the same, Schweikert is probably going to make a connection, if he can, between your going up to Mattaskeet and then finding a body down here—being the first one to find the body here, when no one else is around. Just you and a dead woman."

"Well, he can try to make a connection, but there isn't any."

Balls cocked an eyebrow, staring at me. I knew he'd return to whatever his thought was on that.

He was quiet a moment as the waitress came back and asked if there was anything else. We said no and she thanked us and laid the check between us. I picked it up. Balls continued to study his mostly empty coffee mug. "I've talked with deputies Dorsey and Wright. Gotten their version of what was found at the scene in Buffalo City. You tell me everything you saw, your impression, who else came up."

I spent the next several minutes going over in detail my arrival at Buffalo City to go kayaking, discovering the body, what it looked like, who else arrived after I was there. Balls nodded from time to time but didn't interrupt me. The waitress started back with the coffee pot and we waved her away.

When I was finished with my narration, Balls sighed, and glanced at his watch. "We might as well head on down to Manteo."

"What about the victim, the woman at Buffalo City?

You said she'd been identified."

We both got up. I put some bills on the table for a tip. Balls spoke quietly, "Her name was Sharon Dawson. She had no family here. Worked at several places as a waitress . . . and was apparently what we politely call a 'fun-loving gal.' We'll know more later."

I paid the check with Linda up front. She asked if everything was all right and I said it was fine. Balls and I stepped out on the front porch of the restaurant. I could tell he mulled something over in his mind. He turned to me. "What I want you to do is this. Think back over your trip to Mattaskeet, everybody you met, everybody you saw or who saw you, your impression of the situation there, whether there was anyone of interest there . . . everything. Write it down, if necessary, and tell me everything later. Every detail. Think about it, carefully, every detail."

He walked to his car and I turned toward mine, parked two spaces away. He nodded toward my Subaru. The old grin came back. "Well, I see you got rid of that Snob and got you a more practical vehicle."

"It was a Saab, Balls."

"Oh, yeah. That's right." He stood there with his hand on the door to his Thunderbird, gazing off toward the ocean. There was something else he wanted to say. I waited. He turned back to me. "I know you don't believe in coincidences. I don't hardly either. So maybe, just maybe, it wasn't an accident—a coincidence—that you were the one who found the body at Buffalo City." He cocked that eyebrow at me again. "Maybe, just maybe, somebody was sending you a message. They wanted you to be the one who found the body."

I didn't say anything.

"Think about it," he said.

He knew I would. I knew it too.

Chapter Five

I followed Balls to Manteo. He stuck fairly close to the fifty miles-per-hour speed limit most of the way. He edged it up a bit in the stretch just before Jockey's Ridge, and he gunned it nicely going over the Washington Baum Bridge at Roanoke Sound. He parked in a reserve spot at the old Dare County Courthouse and I found a convenient spot on Sir Walter Raleigh Street around the corner.

Balls waited for me on the front porch of the courthouse. He nodded toward the window to the Register of Deeds office just inside on the left. That's where Elly works. Balls had that grin on his face. "Want to go in and speak to your sweetie before going upstairs to see Schweikert? A little sugar before something sour?"

I made a face at him. "Come on, Balls. Let's get this over with."

As we passed Elly's door I saw her standing behind her desk talking to an elderly man who stood with his back to us. She had a pleasant smile on her face. She saw us out of the corner of her eye and nodded slightly, the smile still there.

Upstairs we met Mabel. She was coming out of the sheriff's office with a file, shuffling along the hallway in her cushioned black shoes, limping a bit on those swollen ankles she's suffered with for decades. Mabel greeted us, but then cast her eyes heavenward and tilted her head toward the sheriff's office. "They're expecting you," she said. I knew that Schweikert was not one of her favorite people either.

Balls tapped lightly on the sheriff's door and we stepped inside. Sheriff Eugene Albright sat at his desk like a big bear. He half-rose when we came in, then settled back in his chair with a sigh, like air going out of an inner tube. Across from the sheriff sat District Attorney Rick Schweikert. As usual, he wore a stiffly starched white dress shirt and tie. We all knew he pressed his shirts himself because he trusted neither the laundry nor his wife to do them up to suit him. His reddish blond hair was clipped short, his face shiny. He nodded curtly at Balls and me.

Balls had started toward the chair at the end of Albright's desk when Schweikert spoke. He glared at me but tilted his head briefly toward Balls. "I see you brought your bodyguard with you," Schweikert said.

Balls stopped in mid-stride. He took a deep breath, letting it out slowly before he spoke, staring down at Schweikert: "Let's get something straight, Schweikert. I'm the investigator on his case—the chief investigator. I have business here. As for you, your job doesn't even start until there's an arrest and a trial." He continued staring down at Schweikert, who seemed to shrink ever so slightly back into his chair. "You got it?"

"Sure. No offense intended."

"Right," Balls said. Then he went to his chair, sat, and tilted it back a bit, his feet flat and firmly on the floor.

I took the straight-back chair at the other end of the sheriff's desk.

"Now, gentlemen," Sheriff Albright said, "let's just keep it pleasant, and informative. We're here to sort of layout the groundwork on this investigation, and since Mr. Weaver here was the first one to discover the body, we thought it sensible to start with what he may have observed when he got there."

Schweikert spoke up. "And what he was doing there."

"I was prepared to go kayaking," I said.

Schweikert shook his head, a mock look of sadness turned his thin lips downward. "I'm just amazed, Mr. Weaver, how you can always just *happen* to be around when a body is discovered—and you've then got something else to write about."

I could see that Balls squirmed to keep himself under control and not lash out again at Schweikert.

Sheriff Albright held his big palms up, signaling to cool it. "Go ahead, Mr. Weaver."

I recounted how I had arrived at Buffalo City shortly after dawn and found the woman's body as I approached the launching area, even before I had taken my kayak off the roof of my Subaru. This was the second time Balls had heard me tell about finding the body, and I knew he listened carefully for anything that hadn't come up the first time.

When I had finished detailing the story, including names of the deputies who were the first to arrive, about the couple from Maryland and other potential kayakers, Schweikert asked, "Did you know this young woman?"

"No," I said. "There was something familiar about her, as if maybe I had seen her around town. But no, I did not know her."

Balls remained quiet, as did the sheriff.

"How do you think she was killed?" Schweikert asked.

"When I first approached her, I logically assumed she had been strangled because she was hogtied."

"When you first approached her?"

"Yes. But after I looked at her facial features, I wasn't sure. She didn't look like she had been strangled."

"What do you mean? You something of an expert on how someone looks who's been strangled?"

"No. I'm not an expert, but . . . "

Balls interrupted. "Let's don't play games. We have the prelim on the autopsy and it bears out what Weav was just saying."

The sheriff picked up a sheet of paper on his desk, just glanced at it because I was sure he had read it carefully earlier. "Apparently she was already dead when she was tied up the way you found her. She had been heavily drugged and then probably smothered with something like a pillow while she was unconscious."

I nodded. I knew now was the time for Schweikert to bring up the death in Mattaskeet. But he didn't. Silence hung in the room for a moment or two. Then Balls spoke: "I'll be talking to some of the folks where she worked." He consulted a small spiral notebook he pulled from his breast pocket. "See who she was friendly with. Who she ran with."

I waited to see if he would mention where she had worked. I was thinking I might have seen her at one of those places.

"Agent Sam Doughtry handled the notification with the victim's mother in Greenville," Balls said. "Seems the mother is about the only relative we could find. He'll follow up on anyone there she might have had a relationship with. But I think she'd been around here for a few years."

Sheriff Albright sighed again and shook his head. "We don't need anything like this around the county. We really don't. Bizarre, too."

Schweikert had been uncustomarily quiet. "Bizarre is right," he said. "Apparently she was killed somewhere else and then taken all the way to Buffalo City and dumped. Why?" That smirk of his came back over his face. "Just so Mr. Weaver here could find her?"

I knew, of course, that Schweikert was just being his usual sarcastic self, but of course that thought nudged against my mind as a weird possibility, especially after Balls' comment at breakfast along the same line.

Balls shook his head. "We don't know where she was killed. You say 'taken all the way to Buffalo City,' but we don't know that. Maybe she was killed in a parked car right there at Buffalo City." We talked on for several more minutes without covering any new intelligence. Then Balls stood, flexed his big shoulders, and said, "If you gentlemen are through talking with Weav, I think I'll head on out and get to work. Lots of folks I want to talk to—that'll probably tell me more than he has." Balls nodded toward me.

I stood also. "Sheriff," I said, and nodded a goodbye. I inclined my head toward Schweikert. "Always . . . always interesting, Rick," I said.

Schweikert didn't get up, just glared at me.

I followed Balls into the hall and downstairs. I didn't see Elly in her office as we passed. We stood on the front porch of the courthouse before Balls spoke. "Interesting he didn't bring up something about the story you were supposed to be working on up at Mattaskeet—that other gal hogtied, and probably dead before she was trussed up."

"Maybe he doesn't know I went up there."

"He probably knows." Balls stared off toward the waterfront. "It'll come up, I suspect. Sooner or later." He stuck one of his big paws out to shake hands. "I'll be in touch." He took a step away.

"Where'd she work?"

He stopped. "Huh?"

"The victim. Sharon Dawson. Where'd she work?"

"She waitressed around. Several places. Lone Cedar, at Sugar Creek, even Duck Woods Country Club." He grinned at me. "But you leave that to me. Don't go poking your nose around." He raised one finger toward the Register of Deeds office. "You just hang around with your sweetie and leave the nosing around to me."

He stepped down off the porch but turned back to me. "Remember what I said about going over your experiences up in the mountains. Then fill me in on anything that strikes you."

"I will," I said.

"Now go take Elly to lunch." He glanced at his watch. "Or at least midmorning coffee." He was gone.

Actually, getting Elly out for a cup of coffee sounded like an excellent idea.

But it didn't work out. She had a meeting with her boss and then had to run an errand for her mother at lunch. I decided I might as well head back toward the beach. In fact, I reasoned, since it was a lovely day in mid-May, with the wind down, the sun out bright in a Carolina blue sky, I might spend an hour or so at the beach in Kill Devil Hills going over in my mind everything connected with the abortive story trip to Bloody Mattaskeet. Too, I vowed to call my editor about the Buffalo City victim. Rose would get excited about the possibility of a connection, seeing it all as a lot more involved story than a magazine piece, possibly even another book. So maybe my trip to Mattaskeet would not be all that wasted—in the long run.

Chapter Six

I cut over from the Bypass to the Beach Road—or Highway 12—once I got up as far as Kitty Hawk. This early in the season I knew I could park at the sandy unloading area just south of the Hilton Garden as long as I stayed up on the wooden lookout near the car. Parking was supposed to be limited to five minutes but I was right in assuming that no one else would be there.

Taking my notebook so I could jot down any impressions of Mattaskeet that I wanted to relay to Balls, I walked up the gently sloping wooden pathway to the deck overlooking the beach—and the great Atlantic. Even though the tide was out and the light wind came from the west behind me, flattening the ocean, the surf's audible power was constant, so constant that at times you forgot that its roar was there. I sat on one of the benches, looking out toward the ocean, and watched the low surf churn brown sand and recede, over and over. A few stiff-legged sandpipers chased the surf.

This setting was a far cry from a month ago on that April afternoon when I had pulled into the little town of Mattaskeet, high in the mountains of North Carolina. Here at the beach I smelled the faint saltiness in the air. There in Mattaskeet, stepping out of my car on the main street, I breathed in the scent of cedar, fir and pine. The air was brisk and I felt good. I flexed my shoulders to loosen the muscles.

I had driven beyond Winston-Salem the first day, not pushing it too much, and then had driven the rest of the way to Asheville and beyond to Mattaskeet starting that morning.

In the sparse downtown of Mattaskeet, there was the main road and several side streets to the left and right: A hardware store, two cafes, an insurance office, and a building with raised letters above its doorway proclaiming "Professional Building," housing a few of the county's lawyers, presumably. There was very little traffic, either vehicular or pedestrian. An elderly woman with a young girl of five or so in tow came by me on the sidewalk. The woman sized me up as a stranger, but the little girl almost smiled.

Mattaskeet County building was a bit farther down the main street. I strolled toward the building. It had a brick façade but the back section of it was white frame. Just inside the main front door there was a white sign with black letters that said "Sheriff's Office." I went in. A deputy, serving as dispatcher, was seated behind a low counter. There was a wooden bench, not unlike a church pew against one wall, and a picture of George Washington on the wall. Two metal government-type file cabinets crowded a wall behind the dispatcher's small desk. A rather dusty window looked out onto the street. I told him my name and gave him one of my cards. "Sheriff Poyner is expecting me," I said.

The deputy, whose nametag identified him as M. Carson, studied my card, looked at me without smiling, and said, "I'll check with him." He got out of his chair and tapped lightly on a frosted glass door to his right and stepped inside. When he came out, he said, "Sheriff'll see you." He still didn't smile.

I went into the office. Sheriff Edwin Poyner sat behind a scarred blond maple desk. He rose to shake hands. He was shorter than I'd imagined in talking with him several times on the telephone. His cheeks were lined with tiny red blood vessels. He wore a khaki shirt and cotton twill pants of a slightly darker color. A silver badge sagged on his shirt, the points of the star a bit off kilter.

He waved a hand toward a wooden straight-back chair in front of his desk. I settled in the chair and smiled at him.

I was glad to finally meet him in person. It had taken four telephone calls for him to agree to see me. He had kept saying there was not much of a story here with the killing of the young woman, and that no arrests had been made. I had told him I just wanted to talk with him and that my editor always wanted to portray law enforcement officers in a good light, which was true. On the fourth call, he had paused before saying, "You live in the east—on the coast?"

I'd sensed, and correctly, that there was a touch of hostility in the words "east" and "coast." So I said, "Oh, yes, Sheriff, I live on the coast now but I used to live in the mountains, in Asheville, and my uncle was an old Republican city judge in Asheville."

Sheriff Poyner's tone had changed. "You can come on up," he said. We set a time and date. And here I was.

"Okay," Sheriff Poyner said, "how you want to proceed?"

"What I'd like, Sheriff, is for you to go over the case, starting with when the body was found, who found her, and go through the investigation step-by-step. Visit the sites, the scene."

"No arrests have been made," he said, and cocked his head toward me as if he expected me to come back with some sort of rejoinder.

"Oh, I understand, Sheriff." Then I added, "Sometimes these things take time. They can really be puzzlers. I know that."

This seemed to relax him a bit.

He reached into a top drawer on the right side of his desk and pulled out a manila folder. The file bulged with several sheets of paper and eight-by-ten photographs whose edges poked out from the folder. "The victim, Judy Burnham, was found in the back seat of her car just outside of town." He watched my face. I nodded, and he continued. "She was naked—nude—and she was tied up. Hogtied, actually."

I waited. I had my notebook with me but I didn't want to spook him by taking notes until he got more comfortable with me. Besides, I knew all of the basic facts anyway from a file of news clips I had, several of which my editor had mailed me.

He slid the file to the center of his desk. He flipped it open and removed three or four photographs. "These were taken at the scene by one of my deputies. Deputy Carson, the officer just outside there you saw when you came in." He pushed one of the color photographs toward me.

I bent forward, put my elbows on the edge of his desk and studied the photograph. It showed a nude young woman, dirty blond hair, her back arched with a loop of rope around her neck. Her hands were bound behind her, and the rope that looped around her neck extended to her ankles, also bound, with her legs pulled up behind her—typical hog-tieing.

But despite the ropes and the fact that she was most certainly dead, she looked strangely more like she was posing than having been murdered in this fashion. Brushing aside the mental knowledge that she had met a very untimely and cruel death, the photograph could almost be classified as a rather twisted glamour shot.

A few moments later, Sheriff Poyner slid the other three photographs toward me. They were the same basic scene, but different angles. One was a close-up of the woman's face. I was most interested in this one. The thing that impressed me immediately was the fact that she didn't appear to have been strangled to death with the rope. None of the facial distortions that would have come with such a death.

I glanced up at Sheriff Poyner, who watched me intently. I pointed to the picture of the woman's face. "She doesn't look like . . ." I let my voice trail off.

He nodded. "Yeah, I know," he said.

"What did the autopsy say? How she died?"

The sheriff puffed out a "Hmmpf." He shook his head,

and gave a disheartened smile. "This is Mattaskeet County. Won't any autopsy."

"No autopsy?" I could hardly fathom it.

"She wasn't from around here. Her folks came down from some place in Ohio, like Cleveland or some place, and took her body home right away. We tried to find out more but her folks had her cremated real quick."

I tried not to appear to be totally incredulous that no autopsy was performed and that the victim's body was essentially whisked away. I didn't want to start by questioning the competence—or lack thereof—of the law enforcement in Mattaskeet County.

I glanced at the other photographs, while at the same time thinking how I would pose my next question. "I take it, Sheriff, that you feel perhaps this unfortunate young woman had been killed by some other method and then tied up? I mean her face doesn't look like she'd been strangled."

"That's what I thought. Old Doc Watkins looked at her too. That was his opinion." He rubbed his palm across his face. "But as I said, won't a autopsy."

I nodded but refrained from saying anything.

Sheriff Poyner glanced at his wristwatch. "You want a take a little ride? See where we found her?"

"Be great," I said.

He put on a lightweight windbreaker and we stepped into the front office. Another deputy had joined Deputy Carson and was perched with one hip on the corner of Carson's desk. He stood when the sheriff and I came through. Poyner told Carson we'd be back shortly, that he wanted to take me for a little ride to the edge of town. I was sure that Carson, and just about everyone else in town, knew that I was there to write about the unsolved murder of Judy Burnham.

As we went outside I asked Poyner if he'd mind if I took my camera with me. "Helps me when I start writing to remember exactly what things look like."

He nodded, and waited for me while I scurried back up the street to my car, retrieved my camera and hurried back.

He then led the way to a dusty brown Chevrolet that had "Mattaskeet Sheriff" in black letters on the front doors. The inside of the car smelled like old cigars. There was a fairly long cigar butt in the ashtray. He started the car and reached over and put the unlit cigar in his mouth. He chewed on the cigar as we pulled west on the main street.

I turned my face toward him. "Tell me something about the victim, Judy Burnham. What she was like, where she worked, who her friends were, if you would, Sheriff." I looked at the fine little blood vessels on his cheek. Then I watched where we were driving. I wanted to note as much as I could about the town while he talked to me.

He glanced at me, and fished out a wooden country match from his side pocket, struck the match with his thumbnail, just as my grandfather used to do. He tilted his head slightly to one side and lit his cigar stub. He shook the match and tossed it out the window. "She wasn't from around here, as I said." He took a couple of puffs on his cigar, breathed in some of the smoke. "Don't like to talk bad about the dead, but she was, well, she was kind a wild. That's the best way to describe her, I guess. Fooled around a lot, if you know what I mean."

I nodded.

"There were a couple of boys came down here too, with her, or seemed to be, anyway. They all three worked up at Mountain Top Lodge. Waitressing and stuff. She also went out with one of the local young fellows. She was quite a tease."

I thought I could pose a question to him without causing him to withdraw. "The two guys who came down here with her, they still around?"

He shook his head. "Naw, they took off right after she was killed." He inclined his head toward me for an instant. "I know what you're thinking. They had real good alibis that night." He took his cigar out of his mouth, looked at the ash, and tapped it into the ashtray. We had gotten to the end of the main road and he swung to the right, angling up a rather narrow mountain road.

"Matter of fact," he said, "those two young fellows left, and so did the most of the tourists we were beginning to get here." He sighed. "Tell you the truth, that's one reason I wasn't so ready to talk to you about this case. We've had enough publicity about it, and we've just started in the last couple of years to get folks from up north and other places to come here as a vacation spot. You know it's a pretty area, and unspoiled, so to speak. This murder has hurt us."

We wound upward around almost hairpin turns, with steep banks on the right forested with pines, cedars and hardwood trees, and views down into a valley below us. We had reached the top of the small knoll of a mountain, with taller mountains beyond us. The road flattened out, and a narrow gravel road veered off to the right. He braked and pulled into the gravel road. Surprisingly, the road broadened out less than fifty yards into it to a circular area hidden from the main road. At the end of the circular area, a weathered dark wooden one-room cabin sagged at the edge of the pine trees. Behind the cabin an outhouse leaned precariously to one side. I couldn't help but have an image of someone being brave enough to take a seat in that slanted thing, fearing all the time that it would tilt all the way over and them with it.

He swung the car around so we were headed back out. He cut the engine, and pointed with his cigar out the window to this left. "Her car was found right over there, parked headed toward the cabin," he said. "Young folks use this area as a lovers' lane." He chuckled. "Some of 'em ain't all that young that use it."

I got out with my camera and took four or five pictures. I came back to the car and leaned on the door by the sheriff's open window. I could smell his cigar but I could also smell the sun-warmed pine and cedar trees. By all things aesthetic, it was a pleasant, picturesque place, yet maybe because I knew what had been discovered here, or perhaps because of the dark wooden cabin and the leaning outhouse, there was an underlying feeling of gloom here as well.

Staring off toward the woods, I spoke to myself as much as to the sheriff. "If she was already dead, somebody had to drive her up here, or there was more than one vehicle because I doubt if anyone walked away from here, all the way back down the mountain."

"Yep," he said, "that's what I figured." His cigar had apparently gone out. He looked at it, and put it back in the dashboard's ashtray. "We even tried to get some fingerprints off the car, but it was wiped clean. Weren't even any of her prints that we could find. And as far as tire tracks, hell by the time all of us got up here and started investigating, any tire tracks would've been long gone. Besides, it'd been dry as a dog's bone."

I moved back from his door as he got out and stretched, arching his back.

"Who found her?"

"Local fellow. Leroy Dinkins. He shook his head and chuckled again. "I kind of think Leroy's got a still up the side of the hill yonder, or at least some booze stashed up there. He came driving up here that morning in his pickup truck and found her. Scared him to death. He was all hung over. I know that for a fact." He looked at me. "And I know he won't the perpetrator either, as you fellows say, because I know where he was the night before—I had him locked up in my jail for being public drunk, again."

I shook my head. "Any suspects at all?"

"Not that I've been able to latch onto yet." There was a touch of defensiveness in his response.

"Yeah, these cases can sure be puzzlers, all right," I said.

"Now, I did question a bunch of folks, including, as I said, those two fellows who worked with her, and one or two of the young bucks in town that'd been squiring her around some." He leaned back against the fender of his car, stuck his hands in his pockets. "As I indicated, she was pretty wild. Drank quite a bit I understand and probably did, you know, things like marijuana and all."

The afternoon sun had begun to dip behind the tall pine trees.

"I guess we got about all we need here," he said. Then, "How long you plan to stay?"

"Well tomorrow, probably. I called for reservations at Simpson's Motel. I think that's the name of it. But I'd like to go back to your office, if I could, and go over that file. You know, get names of folks in case I need to talk with them at some point."

He seemed to consider this for a moment, and not too favorably. But then he said, "Okay. I can let you go over it." He opened the driver's door. "Yeah, Simpson's Motel. There's a restaurant next door to the motel. You can get a fairly decent breakfast there. But I'd recommend Ruth's Café in town. Meatloaf's real good."

"Would you like to have dinner with me?"

"No thanks. Little lady'll be expecting me home before long." We started getting back in the car. "You know where Simpson's is?" he asked.

"I didn't see it when I came into town, or at least didn't notice it."

"When we get back to the courthouse, you head back the way you came into town, about a half a mile or so, and swing left up State Road 117. It's up the side of the mountain there about three miles."

"I can find it, I'm sure."

"Be careful, though," he said. "It's a pretty curvy road and gets dark real quick up there."

Chapter Seven

Back at the Mattaskeet County Sheriff's Office, there was a different dispatcher behind the low counter, an older man, who appeared to be retirement age. But he wore the brown sheriff's department uniform, and a half-smile on his face. Sheriff Poyner introduced him to me as Henry Caudill. "Henry's been here at the department longer'n anybody, including me," Poyner said. "Henry, you can show our writer friend here the little back office where he can go over the file on the Judy Burnham case." To me, Poyner said, "I got a make a couple of phone calls and catch up on some stuff before I go home."

Henry Caudill led me to a small plain office, equipped with a wooden table and three chairs, an outdated calendar on the wall. I took the chair behind the table. There was a lingering smell in the room of warmed over Italian food of some sort, maybe a pizza, and I supposed the room was used for lunches and snacks, probably more so than an interview room, judging by what I'd seen so far of the investigative process.

Deputy Caudill came into the room carrying the file I'd seen earlier. He was taller than I'd thought at first impression. He slouched a bit and his uniform appeared a little too large for his scarecrow frame. He stood there a moment as if he wanted to talk. "Sit down?" I said.

"Be back directly," he said with a smile.

There was something about him that made me want to chat with him. I sensed that I might get a bit more out of him than I was likely to get out of Sheriff Poyner.

I started going over the file and making notes of people who had even tangentially been involved in the case. A good thirty minutes or more later, Sheriff Poyner stuck his head in the door. "I'm heading on out. See you in the morning? Nine o'clock or so?"

"Sounds good," I said. After he left, I heard the telephone ring and Deputy Caudill talking. From the tone of his conversation, it didn't sound like an emergency. When he signed off, I heard him get up out of the squeaky swivel chair at the counter and then saw his presence in my doorway. I smiled and nodded toward one of the chairs.

"Making any progress?" he asked. "Don't want to interrupt you."

"Oh, no interruption. There's really not a whole lot in here that I didn't already know, except for the names of some of the folks—the two young men the victim worked with, a couple of people she'd dated, and then . . ." I glanced at the file. "There's the name of six or eight people from up at Mountain Top Inn, where she worked." I twisted the file around so he could see the names.

He took out rather smudged glasses from his shirt pocket and peered at the sheet of paper. "Them? They're some of the tourists that was up at the lodge. Ones she waited on quite a bit."

I nodded and brought the sheet back to my side of the table. I started writing down the names.

"I can make you a copy of some of that," he offered, "so's you don't have to copy all of it by hand."

"That'd be great."

He took the sheet and one or two others and went to the copying machine behind the counter. I heard the machine starting to warm up. I continued going through the file. I looked again at the pictures, imprinting them in my mind. If I actually did a story on this case—and I was beginning to have serious doubts about it—there'd be an opportunity to get a few pictures, but not these graphic ones of the body.

Caudill came slouching back into the room and unfolded himself in the chair, handing me the copies he'd made, along with the originals. He had also brought an empty file folder. "You can put your stuff in here," he said.

I thanked him and leaned back in the chair, studying his weathered face. "What do you think about his case, Henry?"

He squirmed down in his chair. "Well, you know, I'm the deputy, not the sheriff, and it's not my job to, you know, get too much involved in investigations."

"I know that. But you been around a long time and you've seen a lot of cases, and I'll bet you've got a good eye on what's going on—or not going on."

He squirmed again, shook his head, and looked up at me with a smile. "Start with," he said, "up here we might shoot somebody, or stab 'em, or even back up over 'em with a pickup truck, but we don't never hogtied nobody. That's not our kind of killing."

I waited a moment, watching his lined face, to see if he would say something else, but he appeared waiting for me, so I said, "Then, I take it, you think this was done by some-body not from here—an outsider?"

"Makes sense to me." He thoughtfully bobbed his head in affirmation, and I watched his Adam's apple move up and down.

I started to comment that it was likely she was killed and then trussed up, but I didn't know whether I should speak of that aspect or not. Besides, if she was killed and then hog-tied, that very bizarre fact could certainly lend even more credence to Deputy Caudill's assessment that it was "not our kind of killing."

We talked more about the locals Judy Burnham had dated, and about the two young men she worked with—whose alibis that they were working that night until almost midnight was borne out by two supervisors at the Mountain Top Inn. Judy Burnham had that night off. Caudill appeared to get more comfortable in discussing the case as we chatted.

Then he said, "I know the sheriff didn't much want you to come up here, write about his investigation."

I smiled at him. "Yes, that puzzled me a little bit, but he finally agreed when he found out I'd once lived up near here in the mountains." Well, in Asheville, which was not too far away.

He said, "See, the sheriff and the town council been making a big deal out of the fact that this is becoming sort of a tourists' place. We been getting quite a few folks from up north and other places, all year round. This murder, though, put a damper on the tourist business, at least in their minds. Some of the tourists high-tailed it out of here soon as this thing happened. Just a few of them left."

We talked about some of the plans for the town—a ski lift, hiking trails, good trout fishing nearby in the fast-moving, clear mountain streams. It was a beautiful area, but the stench of death hadn't brought good publicity to the area, that was certainly true.

The telephone rang again and Caudill uncoiled himself and went to the front area to answer it. Once more I could tell from his tone it was not an emergency. I got up from the table and walked to the front, peered out the window beyond the dispatcher's counter to the mostly deserted street. Darkness was beginning to settle in. I glanced at my watch. A few minutes after six. I referred to my notepad and used my cell phone to call Simpson's Motel to make sure they were holding my room.

Caudill finished his telephone conversation. He chuckled, and nodded toward the cradled telephone. "Ol' Miss Monroe complaining again about the Radcliff boys tooling around in their pickup, speeding and creating a ruckus."

I stood there with my hands in my pockets. "I guess I'd better go down to Ruth's and get the meatloaf," I said. "Maybe see you tomorrow?"

"I'll be here again tomorrow evening," he said.

I was not at all sure I would see him tomorrow. I didn't

feel good about there being enough of a story here to make a solid magazine piece—not beyond the finding of a nude body hogtied, which was certainly strange enough. Once I'd said that, however, any sort of investigation had simply petered out. Only way I could write the piece would be to make the sheriff's office look incompetent. That wasn't the type story Rose wanted, or the kind of story I was that much interested in writing. Cops get a bad enough rap from time to time without my adding to it.

Outside, I unlocked my Subaru and glanced down the street. Two short blocks away, a lighted sign that said café hung over the sidewalk. I assumed correctly that was Ruth's Café, and drove there and parallel parked practically in front of the place. All of the other businesses had closed for the night.

The glass and frame front door of the café was large and heavy but it opened easily. The place was fairly busy with couples at tables. Three booths were off to the left, and a large counter or bar at the back. A rather matronly woman approached me carrying a menu. I smiled and held up one finger.

"Sure, honey," she said. "Want a sit right there?" She pointed the menu toward a small table near the front window.

"That's fine," I said. The place smelled faintly of onions and other foods. It was well lighted and had a homey feel to it. I was glad I had come here.

"Meatloaf's the special tonight," she said as I pulled out the chair and sat.

"Yeah, that's what the sheriff said. Said it was good."

"Oh, you're that writer fellow Sheriff Poyner said was coming to town."

"News travels fast."

"Small town," she chuckled. She had a pleasant face, a tad round, probably from the meatloaf specials. She appeared to have a constant struggle keeping her mostly gray hair pinned back. She brushed the back of her hand at a strand of it that insisted on trying to tickle her left eyebrow.

I noticed that several of the customers watched me. I

tried to look pleasant and unconcerned that I was being stared at. Three young men sat together at the bar with beer bottles in front of them. They watched me, and bent their heads together talking among themselves. They wore jeans and work shoes or boots, and sweaty looking pullover shirts. At the other end of the bar an older man ate quietly.

Across from me, the booths held couples and one small family with two children. Three couples dined at an elongated table fashioned from two of the smaller tables pushed together. Two of the couples appeared to be in their forties; the third couple: sixties at least. They had two bottles of wine on the table. They displayed a festive air about them, and not as serious about the meatloaf special as the other customers. They didn't appear to be locals. I wasn't sure what it was about them, but I guessed they were the "leftover tourists" the sheriff had mentioned. They glanced at me but seemed more interested in their own conversations.

My dinner was brought to me by a young waitress in her twenties, also a little overweight, and wearing jeans and a too-tight T-shirt. She said, "You just want water?"

"This is fine," I said. "Maybe coffee later."

"Just let me know."

Actually the meatloaf was very good, and served with mashed potatoes and green beans that had been cooked thoroughly, with a touch of fatback.

Before I had finished eating the three guys at the bar plunked money down and sauntered toward the front of the restaurant. All three of them eyed me as they went by and just outside the front door they stopped at the window. They chuckled among themselves and glanced back at me. I kept my expression completely blank and stared back at them. They slouched along the sidewalk out of sight.

I did order a cup of coffee from the overweight young waitress. She had a nametag that said Donna. "Just brewed," she said as she set the mug on my table. "Sugar and cream?"

"No, thank you, Donna."

She seemed momentarily taken aback, then glanced at

her nametag and smiled.

"Got some good pie. Peach."

"I'm fine," I said and asked for the check.

Outside, the mountain air had cooled. It felt good. I breathed in deeply. I looked up and down the street. It was vacant, just the glow from Ruth's Café sign and the lights coming through the window. I got in my car and did a U-turn to head back the way Sheriff Poyner had told me to reach Simpson's Motel. I turned to the left on the state road, as he had said, and it really and truly was a narrow mountain road.

I had gone maybe a mile up the dark and steeply rising, winding road, with a high bank on my right and darkness off to the left. I had just negotiated a curve when I slammed on brakes. Right in front of me a hardwood tree, only partially leafed out, had fallen across the road.

I studied the tree's top branches in the light from my high beams. By driving off the edge of the road, I thought I could squeeze by the tip end of the tree. I put the Subaru in park, set the handbrake, and got out to take a better look to assess whether I could get around the tree. I tried moving some of the top branches back to give myself more leeway, but I didn't have much luck.

Studying the passageway I would have to maneuver through, I tested the shoulder of the road to see how much I could move to the left without risking tumbling down the steep embankment. No other traffic was around. The road was dark except for my headlights. I thought perhaps I might try backing up, doing a tricky three-point turn and heading back down the mountain, and some semblance of civilization.

Then I heard the sound. It was a chainsaw's powerful roar. Coming from behind me. The underbrush crackled and then a loud thumb as another tree fell across the road about thirty yards behind me.

I thought I heard laughter.

"Okay, you sonsabitches," I muttered. "I'm not blocked." I got back in the Subaru and put it in forward, and thanked the fact that I had all-wheel drive. The top branches of the tree in front of me scratched against the passenger side of my car. I'm sure I held my breath as I got as close to the edge as I could. At one point I felt the car slip a bit to the left. My heart beat fast. I gunned it and gripped the steering wheel, and got around the tree, and was back on the road. I don't think I breathed normally again until I pulled in front of Simpson's Motel. I was glad to see the lobby lights and sign brightly lit. They were the only lights I could see except for a cottage or two far in the distance on the other side of the ravine I'd just navigated.

I parked in front of the lobby. A man of about sixty, who could have passed for Sheriff Poyner's older brother, greeted me. "You must be Mr. Weaver," he said. Then, studying my face, he said, "You all right?"

"Yeah," I said. "But some clowns down the road chain-sawed a couple of trees blocking the road. Well, almost blocking it."

"Oh my," he said. "Let me call the sheriff's office, get somebody to clear the road."

"Yes," I said, "I'd like to speak to the sheriff's office. I think Deputy Caudill is still on duty."

He dialed the number and handed the phone to me across the counter. Deputy Caudill answered on the first ring. I realized I was a little breathless and talking faster than usual as I told him what had happened.

"You managed to get by okay?" he said.

"Just barely. May have scratched my car getting by the branches." I took a breath and said, "There were three young guys in Ruth's Café drinking beer. They eyed me quite a bit and I kind of think—"

Caudill interrupted me. "I 'spect I know exactly who it was. Those Radcliff boys, funning again. They usually do this kind a thing only at Halloween. Guess they wanted to hassle a stranger a bit." He sighed audibly, "I'm going a call their mama and have her jump all over them. Tell her if she doesn't get them up there right away clear that road, they're going to spend the night here in jail."

Before he rang off, he said he'd call me back shortly at the motel. My room was practically next door to the lobby. I pulled my car around in front of the room, brought in my bag, camera and laptop. I made a cursory inspection of the passenger side of the car but the light was not good enough. There was no obvious damage from the branches of the tree. "Yeah, *boys* indeed, funning," I grumbled, shaking my head.

I had gone into the bathroom, splashed water on my face, when the phone rang. It was Caudill. "Those boys'll have that road cleared and cleaned up right quick. I called Sheriff Poyner and he talked to their mama and put quite a fright into 'em. They'll be hustling right away."

I thanked Deputy Caudill, and took a hot shower and went to bed. To my surprise, I went to sleep rather quickly and slept until shortly after dawn the next day. As far as I was concerned, I had about as much information as I figured I was going to get in Mattaskeet. I had names and addresses of potential sources that I could interview by telephone, if need be. But I wanted to sit down again and talk with Sheriff Poyner, draw him out on what he really thought.

So after a watery cup of coffee next door to the motel and a Danish pastry that was certainly not from Denmark, I headed back down the mountain to visit with the sheriff. Where the trees had been felled, the only evidence was a few branches and leaves off the side of the road. The *boys* had had their fun, and cleaned it up.

The sheriff had just arrived when I got to his office. Deputy Carson was on duty, looking sullen and sleepy. He inclined his head toward the sheriff's door and I tapped and went in. I told him I had gone through the file in detail and wanted to talk with him—off the record if he so chose— about what his gut feelings were about the case. He seemed more comfortable with me today, especially when I told him I would be leaving by midmorning.

But before getting back to the main topic, he said, "Sorry about that little business with the Radcliff boys last night." He shook his head. "They're getting to be more and more trouble. Mostly just rambunctious. Gotta bear down on them more maybe."

I dismissed the Radcliff episode with a shrug, wanting to get to the investigation. He surprised me by launching right into: "I know those two fellows who worked with her had ironclad alibis, but I still think they knew something about it, even if they weren't the ones who killed her."

I asked him about the local people. He shook his head. "This was too . . ." He searched for a word. ". . . too strange, or like bizarre, for one of the local folks."

I thought about what Deputy Caudill had said about "not our kind of killing." I nodded. Then I said, "What about any of the tourists? You said most of them took off after the murder. I think there were six of them in Ruth's Café last night. At least they looked like tourists."

"Oh, yeah," he said. "They're tourists. 'Bout the only ones left. Three couples from different places but they travel around a lot. Get together. Got money, all of them. They meet up at various places they have a hankering for." He twisted his lips in what I interpreted as a dismissive scowl. "They'd seen Judy Burnham up at Mountain Top, where they been staying. She'd waited on them right much. But as far as them knowing anything . . ." He shook his head.

We talked further, and I didn't end up with much more than I had—a case that wasn't investigated as much as it should have been, and no real leads. I thanked Sheriff Poyner for his cooperation, told him I'd likely be back in touch by telephone if I had any further questions. Frankly, I doubted if I would.

Despite how picturesque the place was I'd also had about as much of Mattaskeet as I cared for, as well. I'd call my editor and get her feeling on the story—or lack thereof—when I got back to the Outer Banks. I knew I was kissing off this story, but just the same, there was something about it even then that made me feel it wasn't quite over, that this was only a part of the story.

Chapter Eight

My reverie—If you can call it that—about the trip to Mattaskeet came to an end with an elderly couple strolling slowly up the walkway with a little girl of about five in tow. The man smiled and said, "Granddaughter's a little scared of the ocean." He chuckled. "She says it makes too much noise." The man and woman stood at the far end of the deck, bending over from time to time to speak reassuring words to their granddaughter. But the youngster was having no part of the ocean. She hung tightly to her grandparents' hands and kept her head bowed much of the time.

Low clouds had started blowing in from the southwest. The sun was still out but the weather had turned a bit, as it could very quickly here at the Outer Banks. I realized I'd been sitting on the deck there at Kitty Hawk for quite some time, going over in my mind the experience in Mattaskeet. There were several points I wanted to make to Balls. The most important one was that the victim there at Mattaskeet appeared—no damn autopsy!—to have been dead before being tied up, just like the woman here at Buffalo City. As for possible suspects in Mattaskeet, no one jumped out on the radar screen.

The county didn't get the nickname "Bloody Mattaskeet" for no reason. Actually, I knew that moniker dated back to about the end of the Civil War when renegades from both the North and the South descended on the area, bringing with them not-so-great civil unrest, murder and mayhem.

I thought about the Radcliff boys and their chainsaw episode, shook my head again and allowed a wry smile to play across my lips. The Radcliffs wouldn't be the type that pulled off a murder like that of the Burnham woman.

I got up and stretched. A third vehicle squeezed into the small parking area. I figured it was time I moved on. A young couple got out of their SUV. It had Virginia tags. I nodded at them as I met them coming up the walkway just as I started down. The man mumbled something of a greeting.

I would give Balls a ring and check about seeing him later today or this evening when he was free. I headed south on the Beach Road to Kill Devil Hills, cut over to the Bypass and down to my little house on the west side of the Bypass.

Inside, I stepped over the neck of my bass fiddle, and checked on Janey, see if she had fresh water and seeds. I spoke to her and she made her chirping and head-bobbing little dance for me.

To tell the truth, I was feeling a little at loss, the sort of feeling when you know something needs to be done or thought about, yet you can't quite put your finger—or your mind—on it. Scrambled thoughts about the murdered young woman found at Buffalo City, and all of the remembering I'd been doing about the Mattaskeet experience, seemed to tumble together. I needed to sort them out. Okay, I'd go out on the porch, take a notepad with me, and jot down a list of what I wanted to go over with Balls. List-making always helps sort things out. Maybe it's just the process or maybe the fact of writing down items, but it works and helps clarify thinking.

I sat there working on my list, jotting down notes, impressions, maybe just a phrase or two; then began to start organizing the list, points I wanted to make with Balls, points I wanted feedback from him. Then it occurred to me with something of a jolt: This isn't my investigation. This is Balls' investigation and the sheriff department. I'm a writer and not involved. Yeah, right. Not involved. I found the body in Buffalo City, and I was in Mattaskeet looking into a murder very, very similar to this one here in Dare County.

Okay, Harrison. You *are* involved.

I went inside and called Balls' cell phone. He answered on the second ring. He said he was up in Duck, just finished another interview. I asked if maybe he could swing by my house if he was headed back to Manteo. "I'd like to go over a list of things about the Mattaskeet business, and how it might relate to here," I said.

"Hope you got more than I do," he said, a touch of weariness in his voice. "Okay," he said. "I'll be at your place in about an hour."

I glanced at my watch. It was almost two o'clock and I realized I hadn't eaten lunch. I fixed one of my unimaginative ham sandwiches, but garnished with a sweet gherkin on the side, a glass of sweetened iced tea, and took it out on the deck. Janey chirped eagerly, so I took her cage out there too and put it on the little metal table. The sun was bright and those clouds that had been moving in from the southwest stayed south of us. The sun warmed the pines that grew near the house, and if I listened carefully, I could hear the surf, about a quarter of a mile away. I had to listen in between traffic on the bypass. The two sounds sometimes mingled together.

I was going over my list of notes again when Balls pulled into the cul-de-sac. He swung his Thunderbird around and backed expertly into my driveway, headed out as always. I watched him get out of his car, toss his rather rumpled cotton sports coat back on the seat, give a wave of one hand up toward me and come around under the carport and up the side stairs to the deck.

He nodded and took the web-back deck chair on the other side of Janey. I saw he eyed my iced tea. "Want something to drink?"

"What's that? Some of that sissy artificially sweetened crap?"

"Real iced tea," I said, "sweetened with real sugar."

NOT OUR KIND OF KILLING 61

He made a face of approval. "You're coming along, Weav. Won't be long before you'll even be drinking something besides skim milk. Heck, you might graduate up to two percent fat milk."

I brought him the iced tea. He took a loud sip. "Not bad," he conceded.

"Okay," I said. "What's up?"

"I'm the investigator," he said. "My job's to ask the questions." He grinned and took another drink of the iced tea, draining almost half of the glass. "You're just a dirty-neck newspaper reporter, as you're always saying. But one who manages to get himself involved in all sorts of things you have no business being involved in." It was an ongoing banter he kept up with me. He tolerated me more than most lawmen would have. We'd grown close over the years and there was a mutual trust that both of us respected.

I tilted my head toward his now almost empty glass. "Want some more tea?"

"Sure. Then tell me about Mattaskeet—and the good lawmen up there."

Handing him a fresh tea, I picked up my notepad. He watched me.

"All right," I said. "First of all, we have two females of about the same age, both killed and then bound up virtually the same way. We know the one here at Buffalo City was dead and then tied up. The one up at Mattaskeet was also *probably* dead before she was tied up."

"Probably?"

"No autopsy."

He made a face. "Jeeze."

I explained what Sheriff Poyner had told me, and I went into a bit more detail about what I considered a real lack of a thorough investigation.

"Also," I said, "another similarity is that both young women had reputations as being what's been called 'fun-loving.'"

"Yeah, sort of round heels."

I hadn't heard that expression in years. Pushed over easily onto their backs.

"Neither one had immediate family in the area, and not local. Both were found in remote places . . . early in the morning, meaning they were put there sometime during the night. No real traces as to how they were transported to the sites. In the case of the woman in Mattaskeet, there had to be two vehicles involved because her car was still there, with her in the back seat. Car wiped clean of prints. At least that's what the sheriff said."

"Suspects in Mattaskeet?"

I shook my head. "No, but I'll get to that." I looked back at my notes. "Both worked as waitresses. So they came in contact with a lot of different folks. The woman in Mattaskeet—Judy Burnham—worked with two young men, neither one from Mattaskeet, and they had solid alibis for the night before, according to the sheriff. But he still felt like they knew more than they were telling. At any rate, they were long gone from the area. She'd gone out with some local guys, but the sheriff didn't think any of them were involved."

I told Balls what Deputy Caudill had said about "not our kind of killing." Balls tended to agree, judging by the slight nodding of his head.

Then I told him about the chain-sawed trees across the highway by the Radcliff boys. Balls chuckled, and still half-laughing he said, "Heck, sounds like that movie *Deliverance*."

"I felt about the same way," I said.

"What about other people, people you saw. Strangers in town?"

"The sheriff complained that the killing had scared off most of the tourists. There were just a few left. I think six of them—three couples—were in the café where I ate that night."

"You got their names?"

"I really didn't have much cause to start getting names

of folks eating in the restaurant," I said, sounding defensive.

Balls shrugged. "I thought maybe the sheriff might have supplied names, especially since they think it wasn't done by somebody local."

Then I thought of the pages Deputy Caudill had copied for me. "Wait a minute." I went back into the table and brought out the file. "Yeah, I do have names of about eight or ten people he talked to. Some addresses, but nothing really noted by them, except most of them, I think . . ." I studied the list. "Well, most all of them were staying at the Mountain Top Inn where the victim worked."

Balls didn't say anything.

Then I added, "I do remember that I commented to the sheriff about the six people at the café and he said they were about the only tourists left. Three couples that got together from different parts of the country and traveled around a bit."

We sat there for several minutes not talking. Balls seemed deep in thought and I didn't want to interrupt him.

He stood up and put his hands on the railing, looking out toward the pine trees. "It bothers me," he said. "The whole business." He shook his head. "Too much similarity. Both kinky, too."

He turned and stared at me a moment, thinking. "How many people knew you were going kayaking at Buffalo City?"

"Huh?" It took a moment for me to follow his shift of thought. "Well, maybe half the county. A bunch of us were at the Ghost Fleet Gallery, the Frank Stick Memorial Art Show, Friday night and I talked to several people about going kayaking there, that I'd never been." I narrowed my eyes at him. "Why? What are you thinking?" This was the second time this had come up.

He shrugged again. "Oh, I don't know. Maybe some-body knew you'd likely be the one to discover this body . . . especially since you'd been poking your nose into a similar case."

I know I had a look of incredulity on my face. "Sending

me a message? Why?"

"Who knows what gives psychos kicks. Maybe whoever it was wanted to be in one of your books." He leveled his gaze at me. "And whoever is doing this is psycho."

Chapter Nine

After Balls left, I sat there on the deck for quite a while thinking about the case. Then I shook my head, glanced at my watch and knew I needed to call my editor. I'd been putting it off. I brought Janey back in the house and sat in the little chair by the telephone.

I dialed Rose.

When she got on the phone with her bark of "Yeah?" I told her in some detail about the latest case. Just as I knew she would be, she was excited about the two killings with the victims hogtied.

"Jesus, Weaver," she said, her Brooklyn accent coming across strong. "You attract murders like stink does flies." She gave her deep cigarette-hacking laugh. "How's that for a Southern expression?"

"You still don't have it, Rose. Start with, in the South it's a stronger word than 'stink' and besides that, in the South 'stink'—or the word we'd usually employ—becomes a two-syllable word."

She laughed again, followed by a series of coughs. "Okay, Weaver," she said, getting serious. "You've got at least a double-length piece here, and I'll pay you well for it. Maybe even a book. Probably a book. Yeah. You need another one."

"Calm down. Nothing is solved yet, and it may not be. But I'll keep you posted on it. You know I will."

"Don't get too involved. Don't want to get you shot up again. You're about my best writer and I don't want to lose you."

"I thought I was *the* best. Period."

"Well, okay, okay. Just be careful."

She had referred to a case several months earlier in which a bullet had passed through the upper part of my left shoulder. Sitting there, holding the phone in my right hand, I automatically flexed my left shoulder, loosening the muscles a bit. I'd had three months of therapy on the shoulder from Amy at Outer Banks Physical Therapy, and realized that now I didn't even think about the shoulder most of the time.

We talked a bit longer. I assured her the story was hers, whether a double-length magazine piece or a book.

It was almost time for Elly to be getting off work. I called her at the Register of Deeds office. One of her colleagues, Sherry I think it was, answered and then I heard her say in a teasing, sing-song voice, "Elly, there's someone special here who'd like to speak to you."

When Elly came on the line with a slight laugh in her tone, I said, "Dinner tonight?"

There was hesitancy on her part. I sensed she'd stepped away from her colleagues. She spoke softly, "I really ought to go on home, be with Martin. Haven't seen him since this morning."

Disappointed, nonetheless I did the proper thing and said, "I understand."

"I'd really like to," she said. "You're sweet to understand."

"Yeah. That's me. A cuddly bundle of sweetness."

She chuckled. "Right." Then, "How about tomorrow night or Wednesday? I'll make plans in advance."

"Okay, but I was thinking about some of the nice shrimp down at Sugar Creek."

"Why don't you go ahead. I know how you like their shrimp. We can go out tomorrow—or you can have supper with us at my house."

We left it at that. And, yes, I was disappointed. Every now and then, Elly drew down a curtain, an emotional shade, over our growing relationship—and how I hate that word "relationship." But this didn't seem like one of those times, especially since she agreed to tomorrow or Wednesday. She sounded open and upbeat this afternoon. So, maybe I didn't feel too bad. I decided that, heck, I would go to Sugar Creek by myself and get the lightly battered fried shrimp. My stomach growled in anticipation.

I started to call Balls, see if he wanted to go with me. But I knew he was working and wouldn't want to stop. Besides, I'd seen him twice today. That was probably enough—for both of us.

Okay, maybe I was acting a little like Seinfeld's parents but I thought I'd go down to Sugar Creek now, maybe in time for the Early Bird Special.

The sun was behind my right shoulder as I drove south down the Bypass to Whalebone Junction and Sugar Creek. Already there were a number of cars in the lot. I parked and walked up the ramp so I could look out over the water—Sugar Creek or part of Shallow Bag Bay, I never was sure. The sun was low over the water, which glistened where the light struck it. It was only a little choppy. Seven or eight Canada geese searched the shallows. Two ducks floated near the reeds off to the right.

I went in and was seated on the back side of the restaurant with a view toward the water and the lowering sun. Actually, although a minute or two beyond the cutoff to qualify for the Early Bird, the waitress, who said her name was Trish, said I was close enough. I thanked her and ordered the fried shrimp and sweetened iced tea.

While waiting for my food, I noticed that the waitress who was serving a foursome two tables away, stared at me in between making notations on her order notepad. When she saw that I realized she was staring, she gave a faint, hesitant smile and concentrated on what the diners were ordering.

In just a few minutes, Trish arrived with the shrimp, a

baked potato, cornbread, and iced tea. Once again my stomach growled appreciatively, although probably not loud enough for the other patrons to hear.

Making good headway with my shrimp, I realized that again, the other waitress studied me, smiled quickly, and scurried back toward the kitchen. As I finished the shrimp— and I had slowed down considerably toward the end, but I was determined—and told Trish she could bring the check, the other waitress approached me. I looked up at her and smiled; I hoped reassuringly.

"Excuse me, sir. I know you saw me staring at you, but—oh, my name is Vera—aren't you the fellow what, you know, discovered the body of my friend, Sharon Dawson at Buffalo City?"

I studied her just a moment before answering. She looked to be in her late twenties, maybe thirty. Her eyes were large with a touch of eyeliner. Her hair was light brown and pulled back. She was tall and wore medium-length shorts, as most of the waitresses did, a red T-shirt with Sugar Creek in slanting letters. I nodded. "Yes," I said. "She was a friend of yours?"

"Well, more of what you'd call an acquaintance. I worked with her at a couple of restaurants. I didn't know her real well. But I saw her the afternoon before, you know, before what happened to her." She made a face. "That was horrible."

"Yes it was," I said. "Where did you see her that afternoon?"

Before she could respond, Trish came back with my check. She gave a puzzled look at Vera.

Vera shrugged and said, "We're just talking. About Sharon Dawson."

"Oh," Trish said, but I don't think the name registered with her. I handed Trish my credit card. She glanced again briefly at Vera and said, "I'll be right back."

Vera looked over her shoulder to see if her customers needed anything. "I got a get back to work," she said. "But,

answer your question, I saw her at Tanger Outlet that afternoon. She was in good spirits and said she was buying some
clothes to go to a fancy party that night."

I thought about the fact that she didn't have any clothes
on when I saw her. "Where was the party? Did she say?"

"No, just that it was fancy and she was sort of, you
know, high about it. I don't mean *high* high, but excited and
upbeat."

One of her customers at the other table held up a hand in
our direction. I inclined my head toward them and Vera got
the message and hurried to their table, then disappeared into
the kitchen. Trish came with my credit card and slip to sign.
I put a healthy tip on it and she thanked me. She paused a
moment, then said softly, "I know the woman you're talking
about. Didn't catch the name at first. She applied here, once,
I know. May have even worked here a day or so, but it didn't
work out or something." She gave a little shudder. "Scary
what happened to her."

"Yes, it was. Did you know her at all? Any of her
friends? People she went out with?"

"Oh, no, not at all. I just know who you and Vera were
talking about. Vera may know." She cast her eyes around as
if she hoped someone was signaling her. "You have a nice
day, you hear," she said as she moved briskly away to serve
another table.

I sat there a few minutes, hoping Vera would come back
from the kitchen and have a moment or two. When she
reappeared with the pitcher of iced tea and refilled two of the
glasses at her table, she walked toward me, still holding the
pitcher.

"I'd like to talk to you a bit, Vera, if I could."

She looked over her shoulder. "I'm going to take a break
in a minute. I can see you up front for real quick. But not
long."

"I'll hang around," I said. I weaved around the tables
and went toward the restaurant's entrance and stood admiring the clear, large aquarium near one set of the kitchen

doors. Vera came out, appearing a bit nervous; I figured she was more nervous about possibly ignoring her customers than in talking with me.

"I didn't really know her much. Want you to understand that."

"I understand. But did you know any of the people she went around with? Any of the guys she dated?"

"Oh, no. Not at all."

I was afraid I'd really spook her with the next question, but I figured I'd hung on to her as long as I could. "Vera, have any of the police, or investigators, talked with you about Sharon Dawson?"

She looked positively terrified. "Oh, no." She shook her head. "I don't want to get involved at all."

I tried to reassure her. "There's no chance of that, anyway. It's just that maybe you could be helpful. But don't worry about it at all." Then, in what I hoped would be perceived as an afterthought, I took one of my business cards out of my wallet and handed it to her. "Listen, if you think of anything else, please feel free to give me a ring. And it's just between you and me. Okay?" Well, it was something of a lie to say it would be just between the two of us, but I figured there was little harm in that.

She hardly glanced at my card and stuffed it quickly into a side pocket of her shorts. "I got a get back to work."

"Good to meet you, Vera." As I left, I smiled at the two women at the front reception desk.

As soon as I got outside and into my Outback, I called Balls' cell phone.

A gruff: "Yep?"

I told him about my brief conversation with Vera and the fact that she'd seen the victim, Sharon Dawson, the afternoon before she was killed and that Sharon had been excited about attending "a really fancy party."

"Don't know any more about this party, where it was or anything?"

"Nope."

"Still more than I know," he said. He was quiet a moment, then said, "I did talk with some of the people she's worked with in the past. None of them could shed much light on outside contacts she had, like boyfriends and the like—except that all of them indicated she gave the impression of being sort of wild." Again there was a pause, as if he weighed what he wanted to tell me. "She worked up at Duck Woods Country Club as a waitress, or server, as they say. Apparently she got something of a reprimand there for being too 'familiar' with some of the members. At least 'familiar' is the word that was used." Then he said, "And she didn't last long after that."

I knew I was overstepping a bit, but I said, "Maybe that's where we start. Talking to some of the members at Duck Woods . . ."

"What do you mean *we*?"

"Sorry. Got carried away."

"Just so you know, I've already been doing that."

"I should have known that."

"Yeah. But she worked up beyond Duck at the Sand Pebble restaurant longer than most places. If she met anybody and got invited to this 'fancy party' I have a feeling it would be someone there."

"Why don't you and I go up there to eat tomorrow night?" I said. Then I remembered my tentative date with Elly. Well, we'd agreed on Tuesday or Wednesday.

"You're paying," he said, and chuckled. "Kind of expensive."

Chapter Ten

I called Elly that evening and set a definite date for Wednesday night. She suggested I come over there for dinner and then we would go out Friday or Saturday night for a "grown-up date." I chuckled and agreed. She was in good spirits and that pleased me. According to the movies and a lot of books, I know that most people nowadays fall into bed before the first date is over. I guess we're sort of old-fashioned. She certainly is, even though both of us have been married—and widowed. I don't know, we've come close two or three times but it seems like something has interrupted the spell each time. We kid with each other—both probably just a little bit nervous about making the final, physical commitment—that "one of these days." Well, by golly, it was getting close to being one of those days as far as I was concerned. Maybe that's the way she felt, too. I knew, and she did too, that once that happened, we'd be fully committed to each other.

The next morning I spent almost two hours writing what I knew about the Buffalo City case and how it appeared connected in some way not yet understood to the unsolved murder up at Bloody Mattaskeet.

After snacking on leftovers from my refrigerator in what passed for brunch or lunch or something, I decided to go to the beach and flail the waters a bit, see if a fish or two would favor me enough to get itself hooked on my line. I got my one-piece seven-foot surfcasting rod out of the utility room and the big plastic bucket in which I put a goodly amount of ice, lined with newspapers, a little plastic bag with extra bottom rigs and hooks, a couple of two-ounce weights and a sand spike for holding the rod. I refuse to use any weights heavier than two ounces; if the surf's too rough for two ounce to hold bottom, heck with it. I'll come back another day. I enjoy fishing, but I'm not a fanatic at it.

I had a half-dozen small bait shrimp in the refrigerator and I'd swing by TW's and pick up some bloodworms. They were expensive but they were good bait for spot especially.

The parking lot at the Kill Devil Hills bathhouse had only a few cars in it, so I decided I might as well try there since there wouldn't be many people out on the beach. Midday was not the best time to fish, usually, but I wasn't all that serious about it anyway, and I knew I'd have to shower later and get dressed to go with Balls tonight to that fancy restaurant north of Duck.

Lugging my surfcasting rod, bucket with the bait and spike, I went up the long wooden walkway and stood at the end, studying the waves. I looked for a section of surf where the waves didn't have as much of a tendency to break. That would indicate something of a hole, or deeper spot. About thirty yards north of where I stood, there was a break in the surf as the waves moved in. I trudged up there in the deep sand. A bit awkward walking until I got to the hard packed sand close to the surf.

I set up shop. No other beach-goers within twenty yards. Good. Baiting up, I kicked off my ratty old white sneakers and waded out to the edge of the surf. The water was cold and it took a moment or two to get used to it on my bare legs. I stood only a few feet into the surf and kept an eye on the waves as they came in. I use a sidearm cast rather than overhead. I've found I have more accuracy and can get the line out just about as far. The weighted and baited hooks— one with shrimp and one with half a bloodworm—made a nice little plop out in the ocean straight in front of me.

I had fished only a few minutes when I felt a sharp strike

on my line. I set the hook and reeled in a fat croaker that had taken the bloodworm. Unhooking him, I eased him back in the surf, re-baited and cast out again. No action for several minutes. I reeled in and checked the bait, cast out again. Almost as soon as the line was out I got another strike. This time it was a good size spot. I debated whether to keep him, but decided to let him go. Another half a bloodworm. The shrimp still looked good enough.

The next time reeling in, right where the waves were breaking, I caught a pompano. I put him in my bucket. He'd hit the shrimp. I put a shrimp on both of the bottom-rig hooks and fished closer in. I ended up catching three pompanos, and I kept all three in my bucket with the newspaper-covered ice.

I was pleased, and that was enough for today. I could clean the pompanos when I got back to the house, freeze them for later, and they'd be tasty, too.

Our dinner reservations were for six o'clock. I was showered and dressed in semi-pressed cotton slacks and presentable golf shirt when Balls arrived at my house at five-thirty. He actually had on a button-down Oxford-weave shirt and tie, along with his cotton tan sport coat. As usual, he grumbled about my bass fiddle lying in the middle of the living room floor. He made exaggerated movements, complete with facial expressions, as he stepped over the neck of the fiddle. Janey chirped happily at the extra company and commotion.

Balls glanced at his watch and sighed.

"I'm ready," I said. "Let's go."

We arrived at the restaurant a good five minutes before six. Wide wooden steps lead up to the large front porch of the restaurant. From the porch you could look behind and see the Currituck Sound. I imagined, even before going in, that from inside the restaurant the ocean should be visible. Great location. I could smell the pleasant aroma of food being prepared.

"I'm hungry," Balls said. Then, as I started toward the front door, he put his hand on my arm to pause me a moment. "I'm going to be talking to some of the waitresses, I hope. See what we can find out about who Sharon Dawson ran around with. And . . ."

I could tell he started to say something else, but changed his mind and let his thought stay unsaid. "Okay," he said. "Let's go in. It's show time."

Balls gave his name to the thirty-something hostess, who smiled brightly at us, and led us to a table about midway in the dining room. Balls stopped her and inquired about a table for two toward the back, one that would give him a better overall view of the place. The hostess acquiesced, with a smile that had faded only slightly.

The dining room was open and spacious, light and airy. There were a few other diners in the restaurant and several empty tables. One large table was set up with a reserved sign on it. Our waitress approached after a young man had filled our glasses with water. The waitress had a bright smile also. She was in her early to mid-twenties, short blonde hair, a neat little top, similar to what I saw the other waitresses wearing, and thigh-length black shorts. That seemed to be the uniform. She asked about drinks. We both wanted iced tea.

"No beer?" I said to Balls.

"Not tonight." He didn't look at me. He eyed the place, the patrons, and the staff.

After the waitress brought our tea, we ordered: I got the flounder fillet with green beans and substituted a small salad for the baked potato. Balls got the prime rib with baked potato and "all the fixings you can put on it," he said to the waitress. He looked at me. "You're paying," he reminded me.

While we waited for the food, Balls kept sweeping the dining room with his eyes. The waitress, who had told us her name, but which I didn't catch, came back shortly with the food. Balls' prime rib looked good. The waitress said, "I hope you enjoy your meal."

"Can you bring me some more butter?" Balls said.

"Would you like more sour cream also?"

"No thanks. Just butter."

When she came back with the butter, Balls glanced up at her and said, offhandedly, "Oh, Ashley, did you happen to know Sharon Dawson? I think she works here or used to work here." So Balls had caught her name.

The waitress, Ashley, appeared somewhat taken aback. "Oh, no I didn't know her—not well, anyway. She was, you know, something bad happened to her."

"Yes, I know," Balls said, shaking his head sadly. Sympathy practically dripped from his words. Balls opened the right side of his jacket, displaying his badge that was attached at his belt. I don't think I'd seen that badge more than once or twice since I'd known him. "Tell you the truth, Ashley, I'm with the SBI, and we're trying to talk to some of the folks who might've known poor Sharon. See who she went out with, who she was friendly with."

Ashley looked worried and couldn't keep her eyes on us. "I really didn't hardly know her. I think maybe Elsie did. The woman up front. Maybe you can talk to her."

"Be happy to. Thank you, Ashley. This prime rib looks great."

"Good," she said. "Good. Enjoy," and she turned and hurried away.

"You have a tendency to scare folks," I said to Balls.

He shrugged and continued attacking his prime rib. "This is good," he said, and gave that grin of his: "Thanks for the dinner."

When things had slowed down up front, Elsie, the hostess, came back to our table. Standing there but keeping her eyes mostly toward the front, she said, "Ashley said you'd like to talk to me. About Sharon Dawson."

"Appreciate it," Balls said. He introduced himself, and identified himself as a special agent with the SBI. He introduced me by name only. "Trying to find out a little bit about people Sharon knew. You know, who she went out with."

Elsie said, "Well, none of us knew her too well. Maybe with the exception of Jarvis."

"Jarvis?"

"Jarvis Stafford. He works in the kitchen. Sous chef. He probably knows her better than any of us. I think he went out with her some. But you'll have to talk to him. I'm not trying to, you know, start any rumors or anything."

"I understand." Then, "I would like to talk to him when he gets a break."

I continued eating, taking my time.

Elsie looked at our plates. "Don't let your dinners get cold," she said.

Balls took a bite of his baked potato, the middle where most of the melting butter resided. He chewed and swallowed. "Won't let it get cold," he said, and smiled at Elsie. He was being his charming best. "Anybody else she dated, hung around with?"

Elsie seemed to weigh her words before she spoke. "I don't want to speak, you know, ill of the departed, but she, well, flirted a lot with the diners. We had to speak to her about that once or twice."

"Oh, you're not speaking ill of her. We already know she was a kind of a friendly, fun-loving young lady."

Elsie pursed her lips and nodded. "Yes, she was."

"Any diners in particular?" Balls asked. "I understand she was going to a fancy party the night she . . ."

"I wouldn't know about that," Elsie said. She said it quickly, practically running her words on top of Balls' sentence. I thought she sounded defensive, like maybe she did know about that but didn't want to say. Another couple appeared at the front entrance. "I've got to take care of these diners," she said.

As she turned to leave, Balls said, "Jarvis?"

"I'll get him when he takes a break," she promised, walking briskly to the front, that smile most dominant.

Balls cut into his prime rib. "This might turn out to be

more than just a good meal—that you're paying for."

"You think she knows more about that so-called fancy party?"

"No question about it." He peered at my plate. "Don't you like that fish, or whatever it is you got there? Kind a skimpy looking."

"Fine," I said. We ate a few minutes in silence, both of us lost in our own thoughts. I wanted to be present when Balls talked with Jarvis Stafford, so I hoped that break of his would come soon. We took our time with the meal. The restaurant was less busy than I'd thought it would be. Perhaps still too early, and it was a Tuesday night. Maybe that explained it.

At one point I saw Elsie survey the dining room to make sure all was under control, and then she hurried past us to push open one of the double swinging doors to the kitchen. She came back out and paused briefly at our table. "Jarvis will be out in a couple of minutes," she said.

It was closer to five minutes, and still no Jarvis. We had both finished and Balls used a piece of one of the yeast rolls to mop the prime rib juice in his plate. "Good," he said as he chewed the roll.

One of the swinging kitchen doors opened a few yards from us and a tall, rangy young man in a white apron came into the dining room. He stared at us.

Balls reached a long arm across the empty table next to us and pulled a chair toward us. He motioned to Jarvis to have a seat. Jarvis eyed Elsie and she nodded. Jarvis came over and folded himself into the chair. Balls introduced us. We shook hands, briefly. Jarvis acted as though he wanted to withdraw his hand quickly. He had a long face, a wispy goatee. He blinked and squinted repeatedly as if his eyes had sand or dust in them.

"Appreciate your taking a few minutes to talk to us," Balls said and smiled at Jarvis.

"Yeah," Jarvis said. "Got a minute or so."

"Where you from, Jarvis?" The friendly smile in place.

"Here. I live here on the Outer Banks now."

"I mean before now. Where you from?"

"Oh, I been all over," he said.

"I see." The smiled was a bit more forced now. "Reason I wanted to talk to you, Jarvis, is because we're talking to people who knew poor Sharon Dawson, and I understand that you and Sharon were pretty close."

"We weren't real close." He squirmed in the chair as if he couldn't get his frame comfortable. "Oh, we went out some. After work. Few clubs."

"This past Friday night, the two of you go out then?"

Jarvis narrowed his eyes at Balls, an expression bordering on hostility lined his face. "That was the night—the night something happened to her. And I know what you wanna know, and the answer is no. I was working, right here, until getting close to midnight by the time we cleaned up."

Balls shrugged as if he didn't much care. "You could have gone out after that."

"I went home after that."

"And where's that?"

"I told you. The Outer Banks."

The smile was gone completely now. "The Outer Banks are a hundred miles long. I asked you where. You not hear me?"

Jarvis straightened stiffly in the chair. "I'm not being smart with you. I live down in Kill Devil Hills." He gave an address not but a few streets below where I live. "Share an apartment with couple of other guys." He cast his eyes toward Elsie again. "I'm going a have to get back in there," he said. "Oh, and another thing. Sharon wasn't even here that night. I think she was supposed to be but she took off or something." He nodded toward the front. "Ask Elsie."

Softly, Balls said, "I will." Then he managed to get back some of his smile. "You got any arrests, Jarvis?"

"What you asking that for?"

"I can always check," Balls said.

"Oh, couple of minor things."

"Possession with intent to distribute?"

Jarvis appeared taken aback, but only slightly. "The intent part was dropped."

"I see."

Jarvis leaned his frame forward, eager to get back to the kitchen and away from us.

"Really appreciate your talking to us, Jarvis," Balls said. "Just a couple of other things I'd like to ask. That is, you know some other folks Sharon might have been close with?"

Jarvis' thin lips formed a smirk. "You want a real long list, or just a medium list. She was what you'd call friendly with a lot of—folks."

Balls hunched his shoulders a bit as if he didn't really care. "Oh, I can check back with you when you're not so busy, get a few more details about that list of *folks*."

Jarvis stood, "I really got a get back in there."

"Sure." Then, "Oh, you said you were from all over, or something like that. But I'd say the South mostly. Probably North Carolina."

"Yeah."

"West of here, I'd say. Not a 'flatlander.'"

Jarvis bobbed his head.

"Mountains?"

Jarvis shrugged. "Yeah, went to school for a bit up at Boone. Lived in Asheville a while."

At the mention of the mountains and Asheville, I couldn't help but do something of a doubletake at this tall, lanky chef, who virtually squirmed to end the conversation.

"That's all for now, Jarvis, and thanks a lot." Balls extended his hand. Jarvis barely shook hands and loped back through the swinging doors.

Balls studied his empty, wiped-clean plate a moment, grinned at me, and said, "Be sure to leave Ashley a nice tip."

Chapter Eleven

Balls patted his stomach appreciatively as we left the dining room and stood for a few minutes on the wide front porch, breathing in the nice ocean breeze.

"What do you think about our sous chef, Mr. Jarvis Stafford?" I asked.

"What the hell is a sue chef?"

"It's sous. French. S-o-u-s, but pronounced like 'sue.' Means assistant chef, one that sort of cleans up after the executive chef. The number one chef."

"Crikes. Even bureaucracy in the kitchen."

Balls had picked up a toothpick as we left the dining room, or either he had one in his jacket pocket. But he began poking viciously at his teeth. It hurt me to watch him. He didn't do it all that quietly either. "As for Jarvis? I don't know. He may know a bit," he said. "He's not clean, but I don't know, he doesn't seem, well, sophisticated enough—if that's the word—to be pulling off killings like these."

I concentrated on Balls' face. "You said killings, plural. You're making a connection between the two, also. The one here and the one in Mattaskeet. Sounds like you've accepted that."

"Hard not to, isn't it?"

A young couple came up the steps, arm-in-arm. They both inclined their heads pleasantly at us.

"Try the prime rib. It's good," Balls said. He chuckled,

"But the flounder is skimpy."

The young man looked puzzled, as if he didn't know exactly how to respond. But he managed, "Thanks." He nodded. "Prime rib."

As they went inside, Balls said to me, "I like to be helpful."

"Yeah, sure," I said.

Balls tossed the toothpick over the railing. "I guess we might as well head on back."

We had to step to one side to make room for three couples that approached the steps together. They laughed and talked among themselves. They hardly glanced at us—except for one woman who stared at me for an instant. As they entered the large front door of the restaurant, I watched them more closely.

"Jesus," I muttered under my breath. I stood there frozen in place.

Balls turned to me. "What is it?"

"Those people. Just went in. I'm sure I recognize at least one of them, and I think she did me." I took a deep breath. I could feel my heart beating faster, a flush to my face. "Balls, I may be wrong, but I'll swear those are the same six people I saw eating together in Mattaskeet."

"You're kidding me."

I shook my head. "No, I'm not."

Balls stepped closer to the front door so he could see as the three couples entered the dining room. I stood beside him, still not able to accept what I knew to be true. Those *were* the same six people I saw vacationing in Mattaskeet— the last of the tourists, as the sheriff said.

We watched as a beaming Elsie met them and proceeded with them into the dining room, out of our line of sight.

Balls turned toward me again. "You sure?"

"Unless I'm really mistaken, Balls. I noticed them that night in Mattaskeet because they stood out from the other people there. They didn't look like the *Deliverance* crowd."

Balls didn't move. He chewed on his lower lip.

"Curious," he said. "Really curious." He touched me lightly on the shoulder. "You stay here. I'm going in speak to Elsie—see if she found my sunglasses, or something like that."

I paced back and forth on the porch, and kept glancing toward the front door, watching for Balls to reappear. After a few moments, Balls and Elsie stepped out into the hallway by the dining room door. Balls leaned close to her so he could apparently speak softly. She answered him but was obviously anxious to get away, get back in the dining room. Balls nodded to her and she smiled quickly and vanished. Balls came lumbering back out onto the porch.

"Okay," I said. "You get those sunglasses?"

"Yeah," he said. Then, "Stroll with me." We went down the steps to the parking area. Balls looked around at the vehicles parked there, fewer than a dozen, not counting his Thunderbird.

I kept quiet, but I almost squirmed to hear what he'd learned from Elsie, what he saw in the dining room. I knew, though, in his good time he'd tell me. Just the same, it was difficult for me to avoiding asking. I was trying to learn to know when not to run my mouth.

Balls put his hand on the hood of a black BMW. He nodded, "Warm," he said. He did the same to two other vehicles, but didn't say anything. He placed his hand on the hood of a dark-colored Mercedes SUV, and nodded. He pulled out a notepad from his inside coat pocket and jotted down the license number of the Mercedes, which had Florida tags, and then he did the same at the BMW, with an Ohio license.

As we went to his Thunderbird, I couldn't keep quiet any longer. "You going to tell me what you found out inside?"

He still didn't say anything. We settled in his car. He sat there a moment or two without starting the engine, deep in thought. He held his car's ignition key in his hand but did not insert it, just rubbed his fingers over the key, toying with it and staring straight ahead. He took a deep breath. "Okay," he said, "too many links for this whole business not to be connected. Ain't random, either. Didn't just happen.

I wanted to prod him into speaking more freely, but I waited. And waited.

He took another deep breath. "Elsie said those six people been eating there just about every night since last week. And they've got another reservation for tomorrow night. They're staying in Duck at one of those McMansions. Friend of hers is the agent for RealEscapes, rented the place for them—three couples. She doesn't think they're all from the same place but they meet and travel together."

He stared hard at me. "You sure these are the six people you saw at Mattaskeet?"

"Virtually positive," I said.

He nodded, and gazed back out his windshield. "Okay, here's what we got. Those six people are up in the mountains together and a woman gets killed and tied up. Then these three couples show up here, and another woman is done in. Both of the women worked as waitresses in fancy places, and both of them were what we'd call party girls. Fun-loving."

He put the key in the ignition but didn't turn it.

"This local girl tells a friend she's going to a fancy party. We don't know where—yet—but she ends up dead that night and dumped, or placed, at Buffalo City."

He looked back at me. "Where you just happen to find her—cause you're going kayaking there that morning—and half the county knows that."

Balls pursed his lips. Then a smile began to creep slowly across his face, and he started humming—off-key, but close enough that I recognized the tune: "The Games People Play." He started the engine. He inclined his head toward the Mercedes and the BMW. "Going to do some checking," he said, as if I didn't know that.

As we pulled out of the parking lot and started south on Highway 12, Balls said, "Going to be interesting tomorrow when we have dinner back there again—and introduce ourselves to the three traveling couples. See how they react to you."

I thought about my date tomorrow night with Elly. Well, she'd understand. Maybe.

"Meanwhile," Balls said, "I'm going to be finding out a whole lot about these three couples, where they're really from, what they do for a living, and I think we can assume they're loaded. Two of the couples young to be retired, but who knows nowadays."

We drove along Highway 12 without talking until we swung around at Southern Shores intersection and got on the Bypass. Then I said, a clear tone of doubt in my voice, "Six psychos? That's hard to believe."

Balls didn't answer until we had passed Kitty Hawk Road and Capt'n Frank's hotdog emporium, a favorite for both of us. Balls ducked his head toward Capt'n Frank's. "You would've enjoyed a foot-long there more than that skimpy flounder. Or better yet, one of their snap dogs." He licked his lips. "They actually snap when you bite into 'em."

I shook my head. Then said, "Come on, Balls. Six psychos?"

"We'll see," Balls said. He cast a quick sidelong glance at me. "Who knows? Hardly anything surprises me after all these years." We caught a red light at Helga Street. He drummed his fingers on the steering wheel. "Tomorrow night should be interesting." He chuckled to himself. "Meanwhile, I'm going a nose around at the real estate office, check out exactly where they're staying, and make sure our Triple Twosomes aren't planning on leaving the area."

"Their vehicles? Search warrants?"

"Yeah, you're coming along at this DE-tective stuff." He exaggerated the word. "The vehicles can wait—maybe twenty-four more hours. Get a search warrant, if the judge'll stand for it. But we'll be keeping a close eye on those vehicles."

He pulled into my cul-de-sac. It was too late to call Elly about tomorrow. I decided to do that first thing in the morning. I cut on lights and spoke to Janey, made sure she had plenty of seeds and water. "Time to cover you up, gal," I said.

The phone rang. I picked up the receiver on the second ring. I glanced at my watch. Shortly after nine. Too late for most people to be calling. The caller ID was blocked. Late, too, for a telemarketer. "Weaver," I said rather curtly. The line went dead.

I never like that.

Chapter Twelve

The next morning I called Elly after she'd had time to get to work and settle in a bit. When she picked up the phone, I went right into it: "I'm sorry, but I'm going to have to beg off tonight. Balls wants me to go with him. He's got a lead on the investigation."

She was quiet a moment. "What have *you* got to do with Agent Twiddy's investigation?"

Hell, I didn't know how much to say, or what to say. She certainly had a point. It *was* an SBI investigation, headed by Agent T. Ballsford Twiddy. I had no direct connection with the investigation—except that I'd seen those same couples up at Mattaskeet. Or at least I thought they were the same ones, and Balls wanted to checkout their reaction as we—what?—introduced ourselves. Yes, I could see why Elly had a question. So I prepared to do the less than honest thing—fuzz up my answer. But then that old built-in burst of anger that I have surfaced, and I said, "Well, of course it's Agent Twiddy's investigation, but remember, I'm the one who discovered the body, and trussed up the same way as the one up in the mountains. And dern it, Elly, I *am* a crime writer. That's how I make my living. You know that, and you've known it from the beginning, and . . ." I let my voice trail off, and just as suddenly as it came, the anger left me and I regretted lashing out at her.

"I'm sorry," I mumbled. "Shouldn't blow up."

"I understand," she said, but I couldn't tell from her tone whether she really did or not. Then I could hear the two women she works with chatting in the background, and I assumed she had to be rather circumspect in what she said. A couple of seconds passed and she said, "Your reaction was justified . . . I'll see you tomorrow night?"

I wasn't sure whether this was one of those times when she emotionally pulls down the shades on her feelings or that she guarded what she said because of her coworkers. I felt better when she chuckled softly and then apparently cupped her hand over the phone's mouthpiece to whisper, "Just remember you are a writer and not a . . . a gunslinger."

All in all, I felt reasonably good after our telephone conversation to break a date with her that night.

Later that morning I called Rose Mantelli to fill her in a bit. I told her that developments here helped confirm there might definitely be a link between the murder up at Mattaskeet and the one here on the coast. She wanted to know more details but I told her I would tell her more as it developed, and if it developed. But at the moment, I said, it is looking promising for one heck of a story, maybe even another book.

I knew I might be overselling the situation, but I did have a feeling that we were on to something. And I realized that there I was again thinking "we" as far as the investigation was concerned. I knew I had an almost impossible time staying uninvolved. I had come to grips with this facet of my personality or mindset over the past couple or three years. I do relish unraveling the puzzle of an investigation. Too, I burn to have the guilty sonsabitches involved put away—or put under.

By five-thirty that afternoon I was dressed and ready to go with Balls back to the restaurant in Duck, introduce ourselves to the traveling sextet. I was getting ready to play scales on the bass when Balls pulled into the cul-de-sac, turned around and backed into my driveway. I laid the bass down and stepped out on the deck and greeted him.

As he lumbered up the outside stairs and came in through the side door that opens onto the kitchen/eating area, I came back in. He glanced at my bass lying on its side on the living room floor. "Still can't pick up that cello, can you?"

"It's a bass, Balls," I said, once again.

"Whatever." He jiggled his car keys, and inclined his head toward the door. "You ready to go?"

He drove up Duck Road, holding it to only a shade above the forty-five miles-per-hour speed limit, and he stayed close to the lower speeds posted in Duck. He gave me something of a fill-in as we made the twenty-something minute trip.

"Okay," he said, casting his eyes quickly toward me and then back to the road, "here's the plan for tonight." He hesitated a moment and pursed his lips, as if he wanted to start over again.

"Yeah?" I queried when he didn't continue.

He frowned. I knew the frown was directed at me. "I did do some checking. I know where they're staying. Separate apartments in one of those great big houses." He gave me the exact address and I etched it into my memory. "Found that out last night from the hostess, and confirmed it. All three couples registered for another eight days. They travel together. At least meet up together." He turned a grin toward me. "And, yep, they did come here after a stay in the mountains."

I was right! My heart beat faster. They *were* the same people I saw in Mattaskeet County. There had to be a link to what happened. There just *had* to be. My thoughts whirled around, trying to grasp it, make some sense of it all.

Balls glanced over at me, studied my expression for a moment, and then had to brake suddenly for an SUV that eased out of a side street in front of us. A man and woman were in the front seat with about three kids bouncing around in the back. The man, who drove, appeared to be looking for something. Then, without giving a turn signal, he turned left into the parking lot of a mini-mart. Balls shook his head. "Well, they do bring in the tourist dollars," he said, obviously referring to the SUV.

He kept an eye on the relatively light traffic as he talked. "As I said, here's the plan tonight. We'll get there a bit before the three couples do. Take our time eating. When they're finishing up, the two of us are going to go over to their table and introduce ourselves. You'll say you thought you recognized them. Whether they invite us or not, we're going to pull up chairs and join them." He chuckled. "Do a little chatting with them." He inclined his face toward me. "Leave that chatting business to me." We approached the restaurant's parking area. "You just smile and try to look innocent and friendly."

He parked, leaving several spaces separating his from the nearest vehicle. As we got out of his Thunderbird, Balls gazed up at the restaurant. "Heck, this is a fancy place, Weav. Probably need dinner music. You could maybe get a job, you know, playing cello for your supper."

"It's a bass."

He chuckled. "Yeah."

Balls was in good spirits. Me? I was a little apprehensive about confronting the three couples, nervous about what might unfold. I felt in my guts that they were involved. How, I wasn't sure. Murderers? One or more or all of them? While I mentally fretted, I could tell that Balls was looking forward to our encounter with the couples. He liked the thought of facing off with them.

We stepped up on the wide wooden porch. Balls took a deep breath, squared his massive shoulders, and grinned. "Well, let's see if Elsie, our friendly hostess, will lead us to a table."

Elsie stood at a podium in the doorway to the restaurant off on our left, the practiced smile lighting up most of her face. "Welcome," she said.

Balls said, "Twiddy. You have our reservations."

"Oh, yes, Mr. Twiddy. Right this way." Carrying two

menus retrieved from the podium, she led us to a table near the center. "This okay?"

Balls glanced round, saw the longer table set for six, and nodded toward a table at the side that would give us a better view of the table for six and the rest of the dining room. "How about over there?" he said.

"Surely," Elsie said, appearing to force her smile a bit. "Ginger will be your server."

"Ashley's not here tonight?" Balls said.

Elsie seemed mildly surprised that Balls would remember the waitress' name of the night before. I wasn't surprised. Not at Balls. He took in everything and remembered everything. Including the fact that I played bass, not cello.

"No, Ashley's off tonight."

Ginger, dressed in a black skirt and short-sleeve white cotton blouse, approached with two glasses of ice water, a lemon wedge on the lip of the glasses. She smiled happily, introduced herself, and asked to take our drink orders. We both ordered sweet tea at almost the same time. I looked up and admired her reddish hair. "Your parents named you appropriately," I said.

She touched her medium-length hair lightly with her fingertips, and blushed a bit, the scattering of light freckles on her face glowing. "It runs in the family," she said. "I'll be right back with your tea."

While she was gone, Balls and I just glanced at the menus. Ginger returned with the two tall glasses of iced tea. We both ordered the prime rib, medium rare, with baked potato and side salad.

Balls immediately opened two packets of sugar and dumped the contents in his tea and began stirring with the blade of his knife.

"That's already sweet," I said.

He ignored me and kept stirring and studied the sugar that swirled in the bottom of his glass. "Good to see you're gonna actually eat some he-man food," he said.

"I figured I might need a little extra protein tonight," I

said.

He grinned at his glass, took a sip, and smacked his lips. "Good tea," he said.

As we waited for our food, Balls glanced around the dining room. Only a handful of other customers were seated, and none too near us. There was a young couple with two preteen children, two elderly women who ate quietly alone, a foursome of two men and two women. Others began to arrive. Elsie seated a man and woman in their twenties at the table she had originally guided us to.

Ginger stopped by our table on her way to wait on the young couple. "Your food will be right out," she said. Then she noticed the empty packets of sugar by Balls' glass. "The tea not sweet enough?"

"It's fine," he said.

She nodded and hurried to the other table.

Balls nudged me with his elbow. He cut his eyes to the doorway. Here came the three couples, led to their table by Elsie. "Bingo," Balls said.

The couples appeared to be in good spirits, talking with one another as they made their way to the table and began taking seats.

As we watched them while trying not to appear too obvious about it, Ginger brought our food. "I hope you enjoy," she said.

"I'd like a little extra butter, please," Balls said. As she went to get more butter, Balls whispered, "Eat real slow."

His voice low, Balls said, "You pretty sure? Same three couples?" He cut a piece of the prime rib and plopped it into his mouth, chewing slowly, watching my face. Without turning to look at them again, he said, "They recognize you?"

"I don't think they've noticed us yet." They had mostly a side view of me, not full front. I could feel my heart beating faster, excitement growing, and maybe mixed with apprehension, too. If these were the same six people that were in Mattaskeet when that first woman was murdered, and here they are at the Outer Banks and there's another murder . . .

We did eat slowly. At least I ate slowly. It appeared impossible for Balls to slow down very much. Another waitress, a bit older than Ginger, served the three couples. First, she brought two bottles of wine. They handed her their menus. Apparently they had decided quickly what they wanted, or maybe they knew in advance.

We played with our food as long as we could. The three couples were served quickly. We kept an eye on their progress through their meal. Ginger came to our table and indicated out empty plates. "Let me take these out of your way." As she picked up the plates, she said, "Dessert?"

Balls hesitated a moment, glancing over at the table to see how far along the couples were with their meal. "Vanilla ice cream," he said.

"Coffee?"

"Yes, please. Regular."

She looked at me.

"No dessert. Coffee, though. Regular."

When she left to get our orders, Balls grinned at me. "You're coming along," he said. "First you order real man-food and now regular coffee, not some decaf crap, or latte or something pussy like that."

I shook my head and smiled to myself. But the smile faded quickly when I thought about our next step—going over to talk with the three couples. They had finished one of the bottles of wine and ordered a replacement. I couldn't tell what their meals were, but they were making quick work of the food, laughing and talking with each other as the meal progressed.

Balls dabbled at his large dish of vanilla ice cream, stirring it with his spoon, casting his eyes toward the couples frequently. I breathed in evenly, sipped at my now lukewarm coffee. I held up a palm and shook my head almost imperceptibly when Ginger started to approach with the coffee pot. She smiled and returned the coffee on its warmer at the side of the room.

Balls scraped the bowl with his spoon, getting the last melts of the vanilla ice cream. He reached for his wallet and inclined his head toward Ginger. "This one's on me," he said. "Or at least the state. So I expect you to be helpful in these interviews—mostly by just keeping quiet. Except, you know, how to get it started."

I nodded. I couldn't help but feel the tension. Balls didn't seem to be affected at all. Ginger brought the check and Balls gave her his credit card. When she came back with the slip for him to sign, she thanked us and said it was a pleasure serving us. When she left us, Balls inhaled deeply, smiled at me, and said, "It's show time, Weav. Show time." We rose and made our way toward the three couples.

Chapter Thirteen

The couples didn't notice us until we stood at the edge of their table. Then they looked up at us, expectantly. The older couple had already been served their coffee. The older woman studied me, and in a quick moment smiled broadly. "Oh," she said. "I thought that was you. I said that last night. We saw you up in the mountains."

"Yes," I said, smiling and extending my hand. "I'm Harrison Weaver and this is Ballsford Twiddy."

The other couples put pleasant, if somewhat puzzled, expressions on their faces.

She said, "I'm Denise Farrish, and this is my husband, Dewey. We're from Dayton." Dewey extended his hand across his wife's breast.

I thought D and D from Dayton. I can remember that.

One of the other men gestured toward empty chairs at the table next to them. He was starting to say pull up a chair but Balls was already doing that.

"Do you mind?" I said, taking a seat on one of the chairs Balls scooted over. "We don't want to interrupt your meal."

"Oh, we're just finishing up anyway," Denise said. She had a pleasant, round face that appeared to have captured a bit of sun today. Her husband smiled and nodded, then took a sip of his coffee. He slumped a bit in his chair, leaning forward toward his coffee as if he thought he might spill some of it. His face was puffy and pale. He didn't look to have spent much time in the sun.

"You're the writer who was up at Mattaskeet," Denise said. "Last night when I saw you on the porch I was trying to remember who you were. I knew I'd seen you before." She beamed, proud of herself. "At Ruth's Café in Mattaskeet. You were eating in there and so were we. Ruth—she owns the café, you know—said you were a writer and up there doing a story about that young girl we'd met at the resort who was murdered." She made a face. "Horrible."

The man who had gestured toward the empty chairs put out his hand toward Balls. "I'm Stan Crawford and this is my wife, Becky. I didn't catch your name. You're . . . Mr . . . ?"

"Twiddy," Balls said, shaking hands with Stan Crawford. Crawford was trim and forty-ish, tanned, and dressed in slacks and a green Polo golf shirt. His wife, Becky, had ash blonde hair styled nicely around her tight, but pretty, almost brittle looking face. She was also tanned and trim. They looked like a tennis duo who worked out regularly.

The couple on the other side of the table introduced themselves as Karl and Velda Simpkins. He waved a hand but didn't try to extend it across the table. He had dark hair with a lock that fell casually across his forehead. He had round, rather sleepy looking eyes like a young Paul McCartney. He kept a pleasant expression that didn't change. His wife, Velda, was the prettiest of the women, with brown hair brushed back from her temples and something of a mischievous smile playing around her lips. She sat relaxed in her chair, head slightly to one side. There was something sensual about her demeanor, the tilt of her head, the enigmatic smile.

Denise spoke again. "They didn't solve that mystery, did they? The girl up in the mountains."

Smiling, I shook my head. "No." Then I said, "And now . . ." But Balls nudged my leg sharply with his knee, and I let my words drift off.

Balls spoke up. "You enjoying the Outer Banks?"

"Oh, yes," Karl said, his round eyes taking on more life. "We've done quite a bit of exploring. Up and down the

Outer Banks. We all drove here from the mountains. Like a caravan."

Denise spoke up happily, "Yes, like a caravan. We all have our separate cars." She smiled brightly. "We call ourselves 'The Traveling Troupe from Table Twenty-Two.'"

Balls looked at her, his head cocked to one side, that big grin on his face, but a question in his expression.

Becky, the tanned woman I'd pegged as a tennis player, interjected, "We all met on a Mediterranean cruise. Shared table twenty-two, and became fast friends."

Velda, her head tilted languidly, said, "Not all of us at the table became friends. There were two people there who were not at all pleasant. But the six of us got along well."

Her husband, Karl, said, "Since then, we've all traveled around to different places here in the states. Couple of years now."

"Yes," Denise said happily, "We're The Traveling Troupe from Table Twenty-Two. That's us!"

Stan said, "During the day and some nights, we go our separate ways. Becky and I do some jogging, work out at the fitness center. Denise and Dewey stay pretty close to the big complex we're staying in. . . ."

Denise interrupted to make clear, "We don't stay in all the time, Stan. I was out on the beach quite a while today." She sounded a tad miffed, but she managed to continue her smile.

"True," Stan said, holding up one hand as a peace offering. "And Karl and Velda here do exploring of the area, as he said. We always meet for at least one meal together, though."

Karl poured more wine for himself and Velda. He held up the bottle toward Balls and me.

I shook my head and held my palms outward.

"No, thanks," Balls said.

"Well tell me," Stan said, leaning toward me, "did you write about that poor young woman in the mountains?"

"No, not yet," I said, trying to look as pleasant as possible. I figured we'd get around to that topic, but I knew Balls wanted to steer the conversation his way.

"Oh, you know we met her," Denise said, her face showing concern and sympathy. "She waited on us there at the resort quite a few times. She was real friendly."

Becky, our tennis lady, fingered her wine glass. "*Very* friendly," she said. She glanced at her husband Stan. "You could say 'flirty,' as a matter of fact."

Stan shrugged, looked a bit sheepish, I thought.

Denise sat straighter in her chair, her bosom thrust out, "And now I've heard on the news that there's been a murder of a young woman here at the Outer Banks. Well, near the Outer Banks. I don't know what is happening in the world today. Just terrible. You go to peaceful places and you expect things to be peaceful."

Balls pursed his lips, cast his eyes momentarily at the table in front of him, and then swept his gaze around at the couples. I knew he was watching their reactions as he said, "This young woman who was slain and found over on the mainland worked here at this nice restaurant."

"What?" Denise exclaimed, a look of alarm on her face. Her voice was loud enough that some of the other diners glanced our way.

For the first time, her husband, Dewey, straightened up in his chair and became animated. "You mean she worked here? A waitress?"

"She worked *here*?" Stan said, his tanned brow wrinkled as if he couldn't believe it.

Karl and Velda shook their heads, sad expressions on their faces as though it was too much to take in.

Balls nodded. "Yep," he said. He reached his right hand into the inside top pocket of his jacket and pulled out a picture. It was a head shot of Sharon Dawson, the woman I'd discovered at Buffalo City. I only got a glimpse of the photograph and I couldn't tell whether it was from her driver's license or a close-up of her face made at the scene. Balls held the picture, it's back to me, and slowly rotated it in front of each of the couples. There were collective gasps, mutterings of "Oh, my God, it *is* the woman who worked here."

Denise appeared on the verge of tears, her voice breaking, as she said, "She waited on us several times. Oh, a nice young woman, so pleasant and outgoing."

Stan glared at Balls, his eyes above the picture, boring into Balls' face. "Just who are you? I know your name, but *who* are you?"

Balls eased back the side of his jacket, exposing the badge on his belt. "I'm with the State Bureau of Investigation," he said evenly.

Stan's voice kept that hard edge to it. He said, "So what are you doing? Are you questioning us, for God's sake, about that girl? Huh?"

"Oh, my," Denise said.

Her husband, Dewey, set his coffee cup back in the saucer with an audible clack.

Balls kept the pleasant smile on his face. "Oh, no, not questioning. Just chatting with folks who might have known Sharon Dawson, or had some contact with her. That's all."

Anger remained on Stan's face. His wife's face became even more brittle, her lips drawn tightly.

I looked at Karl and Velda. They seemed faintly amused by Stan's anger and the exchange that was taking place. Karl's eyes remained round and Paul McCartney-like; Velda continued the self-assured languid expression.

Stan wasn't letting it go. "Well, I can tell you that we didn't know the unfortunate young woman, aside from seeing her in here a few times, waiting on us."

Balls shrugged. "As I said, just checking with folks who might have seen her, talked with her. Trying to figure out what happened to her."

Dewey pushed his cup and saucer away from him and leaned forward, speaking forcefully for the first time. "Wait a minute. Are you talking to us, not just because of this woman, this Sharon whatever her name, but because we were up there in the mountains when that other young woman was killed?" He bobbed his head a couple of times as if confirming what he had just said. "That's it, isn't it?" He gave a half deprecatory laugh. "That's it, isn't it?" he repeated.

"Oh, my," his wife said.

Balls continued his smile. "Well, you'll have to admit, Mr. Farrish, it is interesting that you folks were around when both of these two—" He looked at Stan. "—when these two unfortunate young women get themselves killed." Balls shrugged dismissively. "And you good folks happen to at least speak to them when they waited on you."

"Now, just a minute there Mr. Twiddy, or *Agent* Twiddy I guess it is," Karl spoke up for the first time, but he still had that sleepy look to his eyes. "The fact that we happened to be in the vicinity when these two women were…were killed doesn't really warrant, well, warrant much of an interest in us."

"True," Balls said. "I agree with you." That grin came back with full force. "But you gotta admit it is, like I said, 'interesting.' Fact is, I don't happen to know anyone else who was around talking to both of these women—four hundred miles from each other." He raised one eyebrow and turned his face in turn to each of the couples. He pursed his lips and nodded. "Yeah, I'd say it *is* interesting."

Balls pushed his chair back from the table and began to rise. I followed his lead and stood also. "Please pardon us for interrupting your meal. But it was good to meet all of you." He cast his gaze around the table.

Stan, his voice remaining tinged with anger, said, "I have a feeling we may see you again."

"Oh, maybe so," Balls said. "I'm around here a lot, and there're other folks we'll talk to." He grinned at Stan. "But chances are we'll run into each other . . . again." He nodded and said goodnight. I mumbled a goodnight as well.

As we walked toward the exit I noticed that sous chef Jarvis Stafford stood in the half-open door to the kitchen watching us leave.

Chapter Fourteen

We didn't speak until we stepped out on the restaurant's wide front porch. Balls stopped, turned to me, that wide grin on his face. "I think that went well, don't you?"

I shrugged. "You managed to shake 'em up a bit. Especially Stan." I inclined my head back toward the restaurant. "As we were leaving, I saw—"

"Yeah, I know. That sushi chef guy was eyeing us."

"Sous chef."

"Whatever. Jarvis Stafford. He's another guy I want to have a sit-down talk with."

We proceeded across the parking lot to Balls' Thunderbird. The night was balmy and clear. Stars were visible and two small clouds, looking cottony and gray against the night sky, moved westward. I could hear the gentle roar of the surf, only a couple of hundred yards on the other side of the restaurant. I breathed deeply, enjoying the warm night and salty air coming in off the ocean.

I glanced at Balls as we got into his car. He didn't start it right away. He just sat there, lost in thought. I kept waiting for him to say something, give me his take. I squirmed, settling into the seat, fooling with the seat belt. I couldn't wait any longer. "Okay, Balls, what do you think? Those three couples?"

He shook his head, and puffed out a big breath of air. He put his hand on the ignition key. "I'm going to check with

the rental people again, make sure they're not getting ready
to leave the area now that we've spoken to them. Maybe
spooked them."

"You think they're involved?"

He gave a short burst of a laugh, but not one with any
humor in it. "Well, hell yeah they're involved. But how, to
what extent, and how many of them, I don't know. Not yet."
He twisted the key sharply in the ignition, revved the engine
a bit. "But I'm gonna find out." It was spoken as a vow.

He drove along the Duck Road, keeping to the speed
limit, frowning through the windshield. More to himself than
to me, he mumbled, "Data base. See about similar cases.
Dayton area and Florida. Heck, areas in between."

"Florida?"

"That's where two of the couples are from. Mad-dog
Stan, and ol' Sleepy-eye Karl. Over on Florida's west coast,
Tampa area. At least Stan and his wife are from near Tampa.
Other couple's from closer to the sugarcane fields." He
whistled softly. "All three of those couples are loaded.
Really loaded."

I shrugged. "Figured they had to be." I waited a moment
as Balls fumed silently as the driver of an out-of-state sedan
slowed almost to a stop in front of us and couldn't decide
whether he was supposed to turn left or right. He finally
pulled off to the right. Then I asked, knowing that Balls had
done quite a bit of checking already on the three couples:
"How'd they make their money?"

Balls stared straight ahead at the road and recited as if
reading from notes pasted inside his head: "That couple from
Ohio—Denise and Dewey Farrish—own a chain of fast food
places, one I'd never heard of but must be big in that area. I
guess he franchised them. The Simpkins, Karl and Velda,
come from a line of growers in Florida, citrus and sugar.
Lots of sugar. And Stan Crawford developed some sort of
software that doctors and hospitals use." He shook his head.
"They probably spend more in a year just tooling around
with their damn caravan than you and I make in ten."

Balls slowed, checking a sign on his left, and then he swung into a road, nicely paved and decorated with high shrubs and other vegetation. We drove a short distance to the end of the end road. Three large and imposing houses, each with multiple apartments, flanked the ocean, which was just beyond the front lawns of the houses. Balls pointed to the house in the middle. "That's theirs," he said. "The three couples." He turned around, and we headed south on Duck Road.

Soon we were out on the Bypass, approaching Kitty Hawk Road. Couple more miles and I'd be home. "What about tomorrow?" I tilted my head toward Balls. "Anything planned . . . for me?"

"I'll be busy checking more on this case. But I've also got something up in Elizabeth City I can't ignore completely." He grinned at me. "Maybe tomorrow you better try to repair your love life with the Pedersen gal." He chuckled. "Don't know why a pretty lady like that would bother with a beat-up old dirty-neck newspaper guy like you."

"'Cause I'm so absolutely charming, Balls."

He turned off the Bypass onto my street. "Yeah, sure."

I got out of the car, told Balls I'd check with him tomorrow. He said okay but that there was no need to; he'd get in touch with me if he needed any more expert help. I muttered a "Screw you, Balls," smiled and went up the outside stairs to my little house.

As usual, a lamp was on, and Janey chirped when I went in. I stepped over the neck of the bass fiddle and leaned over her cage to speak to her. Got a millet sprig from the bag under the sink and gave her a treat. She bobbed her head in that little dance. All the while I was thinking that, yeah, maybe I'd better try to repair my so-called love life with Elly Pedersen.

I called Elly at work the next morning just before nine o'clock. On the first ring, she answered, "Register of Deeds

Office." I always liked to hear her voice, even her businesslike greeting.

"It's Harrison," I said. "Good morning."

"And how are you?" she said, still sounding somewhat businesslike. I assumed her two coworkers were in the office with her.

Then she asked, "How did it go last night?" Now, that touch of reserve tinged her voice.

"Fine. I'll tell you about it." I didn't really think I would, but it seemed the proper thing to say. "We're seeing each other tonight, are we not?"

"Yes, unless you have another commitment." She sounded like I did have a bit of repairing to do.

"Oh, you know I don't. I thought we'd go out to eat. Kelly's, or the Black Pelican?"

"Whichever."

"Black Pelican?"

"That'd be fine."

"Pick you up at six?"

"Fine."

A pause. "You okay?"

"Yes. Sure you got time?"

"Aw, come on, Elly."

"No, really."

"We need to talk."

For the first time, she sounded a bit more relaxed, a touch of humor in her voice. "Isn't that what the woman is supposed to say? The 'we need to talk' business?"

I chuckled, "Yeah, guess it is."

We signed off. I didn't feel all that good about the conversation, even though she lightened up a bit at the end. I knew she had reservations about how close we were getting; it frightened her from time to time. Maybe it did me, too. But we were drawn to each other. There was no question about that. Just the same, I knew she worried about getting too close, getting hurt again like she did when her young husband died so suddenly. Of course, I'd lost my wife too, and, whether I recognized it fully or not, I know it colored how careful I was about entering fully into a "relationship"—that word again. And another one was "commitment." They sounded as if they were trying too ardently to be warm and fuzzy, like something you'd read about in a self-help magazine. They had been bandied about so often they'd become sterile, meaningless.

I vowed to stop thinking about how things were with Elly and me. Let it work out as we went along. So I fixed another cup of coffee and stepped out on the deck. I examined one of the wooden flooring planks that would soon need to be replaced. A couple of other places on the deck and the railing needed a bit of work. The windowsills too. Oh, well, sooner or later. I looked up at the clear blue sky. Hardly a cloud this morning, a beautiful morning in mid-May. A gentle breeze came in from the west.

Sitting on one of the two webbed lawn chairs, my coffee cup on the wrought iron table between the chairs: Ah, this is living, I thought, and deserved it, after spending most of my "real" working days in journalism in the Washington area. I'd been lucky with the crime writing, including one book that was made into a TV movie, so that now I could devote full time to murder and mayhem. Okay, nothing so funny about that. Not when real people are involved.

Almost immediately my thoughts went back to Buffalo City and finding the young woman's body there. Involuntarily, I felt my pulse speed up, the memory of that moment of discovery returning. And her killer or killers were still out there. Maybe as close as up in Duck, a dozen miles away. In fact, I knew in my heart that I could very well have been chatting with them last night, sharing a table, if only for a short while. Or maybe it was someone else. Yes, the sous chef? Why was he watching us last night?

I shook my head, trying to concentrate on something else—the sky, the ocean, only a quarter of a mile away, or my parakeet, or the bass fiddle, or Elly or something beside murder.

It didn't work.

I gave a deep sigh, brought my coffee cup back inside. I picked up my bass, tuned it, and played a few scales, using full bow and no vibrato. Then I did my usual exercise, the section from Mozart's "Requiem" that required crossing over the strings repeatedly. It was an exercise I had worked on first over a year and a half ago, and it was still a challenge every time, but I was getting better at it, and I didn't cuss as much playing it.

Later that afternoon I showered and dressed in khakis, a golf shirt, and sockless boat shoes, to go pick up Elly. Traffic was light until I got to the fast-food area known locally as "French-fry alley." Drivers slowed, trying to decide whether to dine at McDonald's or Burger King or any of a half dozen other food places. Once I got through that section of the Bypass, and approached Jockey's Ridge, the giant sand dune, traffic picked up and I moved along at the posted speed limit. Tiny human figures, like black insects, moved around atop Jockey's Ridge.

The sun was low in the horizon as I crested the Washington Baum Bridge over Roanoke Sound. The tree line ahead of me and down toward Wanchese was silhouetted like an India ink drawing. And the brush wetlands beyond Pirate's Cove development always reminded me of the back fur of a gigantic animal, lying in wait. I made my way along Highway 64 into Manteo and continued toward the airport, turning off to the left on the street that led toward the narrow little road, with Elly and her mother's Sears house at the end of the street.

I pulled into the gravel driveway beside Elly's eight-year-old white Pontiac. Her mother's slightly newer Ford was off to the right. I got out of my car just as Elly stepped out onto the front porch, as she usually did when I drove up, and raised one hand, wiggling her fingers in greeting, a smile playing on her lips like there was something about me that amused her. She wore a cotton golf shirt, also, and trim beige slacks. Her hair was pulled back behind the white of her neck.

We shared a hug on the front steps and then went inside. The house always smelled good to me, a combination of fresh apples and cooked ham. Her son, Martin, sprawled out on the living room floor, a picture book in front of him, and the television set on but muted. Martin eyed me steadily.

"Say hello, Martin," Elly said.

He nodded, without smiling, and mouthed something that might have been a greeting. Actually, he was getting so he would talk to me from time to time. This, apparently, wasn't one of those times.

Elly invited me to take a seat, and that she'd be just a minute. I sat on the sofa, and spoke again to Martin, who ignored me. On the end table by the lamp there was the usual crossword puzzle Elly had worked on. Only a couple of spots hadn't been filled in. In just a few minutes Elly came into the living room, a lightweight white sweater across her shoulders.

I stood when she entered.

"Ready?" she said.

Martin began to screw his face up. He got off the floor and stood hugging his mother's legs. "I'll be back after a while, Martin, and you and Nana are going to eat popcorn after supper and watch that new movie of yours."

That seemed to mollify him only slightly. Then Mrs. Pedersen entered the living room, greeted me happily, and took Martin's hand. "Come on in the kitchen and help me cook," she said.

We made our exit with no drama. I glanced again at Elly as we pulled out of the driveway onto her little street. "You look nice," I said. "Lovely as always."

"Thank you." She put her hand lightly on my arm. "Good to see you."

She seemed more open tonight. More relaxed with me. I was glad of that. We chatted a bit as I drove through Manteo and then swung left toward the beaches at the big intersection of 64 and 264. She asked about the night before and how had it gone. I gave her a much-shortened version.

Instead of driving the Bypass, we took the Beach Road, Because of housing and motels, and the fairly recent addition of sand dune barriers, the ocean isn't visible from the road except in a few gaps up toward Kill Devil Hills and Kitty Hawk. Still, for us, it was a more relaxed drive than the Bypass.

We found a parking space up close to the entrance at Black Pelican. The front section of the restaurant was originally an old lifesaving station that doubled also as the telegraph office back in the 1900s. In fact, it was from this station, then located on the east side of the Beach Road, that the Wright Brothers sent a telegram to their father in Dayton, Ohio, on December 17, 1903, informing him of their successful powered flights that day.

As we got out of the car and started toward the steps leading up to the restaurant, and holding hands for one of the few times we did that in public, Elly smiled at me.

And then my cell phone chirped. I frowned at the phone. It was Balls.

Chapter Fifteen

"Sorry," I said. "Better take this." I flipped open the cell phone.

Elly nodded and leaned her forearms on the top railing, looking out toward the ocean, clearly visible from the upper steps of the Black Pelican.

Balls' voice came through loud and clear. "Just wanted to give you a heads up," he said. "No similar cases in the Ohio area. But guess what? An unsolved near Orlando. Victim, a young woman, nude—and tied up. Not hogtied, but tied somewhat similar."

I mumbled something, acknowledging the information. "So, the two couples from Florida? Not the Ohio couple— Denise and Dewey?"

"Not necessarily, either way. But quite interesting."

Elly watched the ocean's waves breaking on the brown sand of the beach, giving me privacy.

There was a pause and then Balls said, "I take it you're trying to repair your love life with Miss Pedersen? You better be nice to her."

"Trying to, Balls."

We signed off and I turned to Elly and touched her shoulder. "It was Balls."

She smiled. "I figured." She nodded toward the ocean. "Always fascinating, isn't it? No matter how many times you look at it."

I leaned gently against her, the light wind coming off the sea, caressing both of us. "Yes," I said, "and sometimes I feel like it's what I have instead of a church."

She studied my face. Then she put a hand on my arm and gave a little squeeze. I wanted to kiss her, and I think she felt it too. But not here. Then we had to shift aside a bit as a young couple came up the steps and entered the restaurant. Right behind them, an older couple approached. The man puffed heavily and held on to the railing as he came up the steps. The woman smiled a greeting.

"Guess maybe we better go inside," Elly said.

"Yes, while we can still get a seat on the porch by the windows."

We were lucky. We got the last seat by the windows and we could see the top of the ocean in the late afternoon light. Both of us ordered the individual Florentine pizzas and a salad between us to split, ranch dressing on the side. Ice water, and that was it. "Not the fanciest dining experience in the world," I said, as something of an apology.

That smile came back. "It's fine," Elly said. Then, while she twisted the lemon into her ice water, she said, "You said you wanted to talk."

I was momentarily taken aback. I remembered I had said that on the phone. "Yes, talk . . ." I said. But I couldn't think of what I wanted to say.

Seeing that I was at a loss for words, Elly smiled broadly, almost laughed. "Yep," she said, "communication is the secret for a good solid—"

"Don't say *relationship*." But I grinned big, too.

She took a sip of her water, amusement in her eyes as she looked at me over the top of her glass.

The waitress, a young woman in knee-length shorts and Black Pelican T-shirt, came to the table with the one salad. She hesitated where to put it. I indicated in the middle. "We're sharing," I said.

The waitress looked from one of us to the other and shrugged. "Enjoy," she said, and hurried away.

"Last of the big spenders," I said.

"I've accepted you," Elly said. "Just the way you are." She chuckled. "Not just because you're a big spender." She picked up her fork and examined the salad. "Actually, I've accepted that you're a writer, who happens to write about crime, and often manages to get in harm's way because of it." She speared a piece of lettuce, dipped it lightly in the ranch dressing, and plopped it into her mouth. As she chewed she still managed something of a smile, her eyes sparkling. She swallowed, and then said, "Isn't that what you wanted to talk about?"

"Well, yes . . ."

"Ah, eloquent as always."

"Okay, Elly, what I wanted to say is that I really, really like you, and . . ."

"That's nice."

"And, I want to be with you, a lot. I know we don't use the word 'love' but maybe we should. It gets bandied about quite a bit."

She put down her fork. "Maybe we *should* use that word," she said, her voice almost a whisper.

Just as softly, and staring into her eyes, I said, "Yes, maybe we should."

She took a breath, gave just the slightest hint of a nod, smiled, and said, "You're not eating the salad."

The waitress appeared with the two pizzas. They smelled good.

We ate and when we left the restaurant and got in the car, Elly said, "Well, I'm glad we had that talk."

We both laughed, and felt good toward each other.

The porch light was on at her house, and at least one lamp burning in the living room that we could see from outside. We stepped inside. It was quiet. "Tomorrow's a workday for me," Elly said.

"I know." I shrugged. "Oh, Friday night. Want to go to Kelly's to the show being put on by the Dare County Arts Council? Should be fun. Molasses Creek band playing, and also Old Enough to Know Better."

She agreed. Said it sounded like fun.

We both hesitated a moment standing there just inside the front door. She stood close to me, and I put my arms lightly around her waist. Then I pulled her to me and we kissed. She pressed up against me and the kiss grew. I held her tightly. When our lips parted we stared into each other's eyes. She held out one hand, her fingers spread and showed me that her hand trembled slightly.

"Me, too," I said.

"Goodnight, Harrison," she said, then added: "And I really, really like you too."

I felt great all the way home.

Later than evening, I sat in one of the upholstered chairs in the living room and flipped through the television channels. I still glowed a bit thinking about the goodnight kiss and how Elly felt up against me. I gave up on the television, sighed audibly, and sat there a moment or two, then reached over to the small table beside the chair and picked up the book I was about half through. It was *The Paris Wife*, by Paula McLain, a novel about Hemingway's relationship with his first wife, Hadley Richardson, during those early years in Paris when he was learning to write. It didn't take but a few minutes and I was deeply engrossed in the story, and not thinking of Elly at all. Hemingway was the hero of my youth, and I'd read a great deal about him—plus his work that he wanted published, and not the stuff cobbled together by Mary Walsh and others after his death. Oh, well, *A Moveable Feast* was published after the suicide in Ketchum, Idaho, but that was more like the real Hemingway. I felt like Paula McLain was doing an excellent job of depicting Hadley and Hemingway during that early period.

I was just rereading one passage in the book when the telephone's sharp ring caused me to jump, startled. I frowned and looked at my watch. It was shortly after ten. I put the book down and took a couple of long steps to reach the phone by the start of the third ring. Caller ID displayed a number I recognized as likely a local cell phone.

When I answered with a curt "Yes?" there was a momentary pause at the other end of the line.

Then, "Mr. Weaver?"

"Who's calling?"

"Uh, this is Jarvis. Jarvis Stafford. One of the chefs." The accent was heavy central North Carolina Southern. "You met me the other night when you and that SBI guy were asking about Sharon Dawson." His words carried a hint of drug or booze-induced slurring.

"Yes, I know who you are. What are you calling about?" I wasn't being very friendly, adopting almost the same tone I use with telemarketers.

"What I wanna know is if there's a reward about, you know, that Sharon Dawson murder. If somebody knows something. And like there's an arrest or something. A reward."

"Listen, Jarvis, if you know something, you need to talk with Agent Twiddy or one of the other authorities. Why're you calling me?"

"I figured you'd know about a reward."

"There's no reward. But if you know something, damnit, talk with the authorities."

"No sense in getting all bent out of shape." There was a definite slurring of his words.

"There's no reward, Jarvis, but—"

He broke in before I finished: "Well, just maybe you *think* there's no reward."

I was about to say something else to him, to admonish him to talk to the authorities, when the line went dead.

Immediately I punched in Balls' cell phone number. It went straight to voice mail. I left him a brief message about Jarvis Stafford's call. I knew he'd call me in the morning.

But I didn't think he'd call me as early as he did. Just before six my phone rang.

"Yes?" I said.

"We don't have to worry about that chef Jarvis Stafford anymore, being a suspect. Not an active one."

There was something about the tone of his voice. I sat up on the edge of the bed, holding the receiver pressed hard against my head.

"He's not active at all anymore. He was found before dawn this morning face down on the beach, two bullet holes in his chest, one in his back."

"Jeeze." I took a breath. "Any suspects?"

"None. But I want to hear more about his call to you last night."

"Where on the beach was he found?"

"Duck. Not too far from the restaurant. South of there." There was a pause. "Roughly halfway between the restaurant and that McMansion where our couples stay."

I thought about that. Then asked, "Where are you now?"

"Same area. Coroner's here now. Area's roped off." He sighed. "But nothing."

"When you think it happened?"

"Medical folks will estimate, but I'd say within the past three to six hours. Midnight or thereabouts. Probably shortly after he talked to you about a reward. He had his cell phone in his pocket." Then I heard Balls speak to someone else. "I gotta go," he said to me.

"Balls, wait a minute. Why you think he was shot?"

"Talk about it later. I've got a theory . . . and you do too."

"Call me later."

He clicked off.

I sat there a few minutes, thinking about what I'd just heard. A theory? A screwy one? I shook my head. Maybe not so screwy, I thought. Trying to hit one or more of the couples for his "reward"? Instead he gets hit, and hit good. Three times, up close and personal. Someone wanted to make sure he was dead.

I took a shower, all the while playing in my mind different reasons why it just so happened that Jarvis Stafford, who knew the murdered young woman, and who had shown an interest in watching us there at the restaurant talking with the couples, then calls me about the possibility of a reward, ends up dead twenty-four hours or so later. And shot on the beach, not too far from the couples' rental place. I knew, just knew, there was a connection with the couples. I moved mechanically, lost in thought. I checked Janey's seeds and water but paid little attention to her even though she did her little dance for me.

I wanted Balls to call me; wanted to talk with him, but I knew better than to bother him while he was in the middle of this, the latest. I knew the area was now swarming with police and Dare County deputies. I thought about going up there myself but decided it was not a good thing for me to do. I'd just be in the way. I'd force myself to wait until I heard from Balls. I made coffee and knew I should eat breakfast, but I wasn't hungry. I took my coffee out on the deck. The morning was starting out clear but there was still a bit of early morning chill in the air. I set my coffee down on the table and went back inside to slip on a denim shirt over the T-shirt I was wearing. I suddenly had an urge to smoke one of my occasional cigars. I took one from the wooden box on the kitchen island, unwrapped it, poked a hole in its tip and went back outside with it. I sipped my coffee and lit the cigar. Smoking it made me a little dizzy at first, but it tasted good to me that morning.

Puttering around the house all morning, I made sure my cell phone was fully charged. I picked up the bass but put it back down on the living room carpet without playing anything. I kept glancing at my watch.

It was close to two o'clock before I heard from Balls again. The frustration in his voice was almost palatable. "Tried to get a search warrant for the couples' rental units but Judge Wilford didn't think I had enough probable cause. Crap! She wants to protect the tourists from any sort of police embarrassment. She didn't come right out and say that, but I know that's what she's thinking. And your buddy DA Rick Schweikert is just as bad."

"You think . . .?"

His tone was sharp. "I told you I have theory, and you know it's based on that call Stafford made to you last night."

I waited, but he didn't say anything for a moment. I could hear him breathing as he held the cell phone close to his mouth. Then he said, "I don't want those bastards to leave the area."

"They're still booked in the rental house here aren't they?"

"Yeah. Two of the couples came down to the scene this morning, along with about a hundred other folks. Stan and his wife had been out for their morning exercise, and the other younger couple, Karl and Velda, were with them."

"Denise and Dewey—D and D—didn't show?"

"Naw, but that doesn't mean anything." He puffed out a "harumpf" sound of disgust. "They saw me, and nodded, like we were old friends. Like everyone else, they acted like it was all part of the entertainment we put on for visitors here at the Outer Banks. Oh, you know, a display of 'how horrible,' but all the while enjoying it. Have something to tell the folks back home." I could tell he paced back and forth as he talked, using me as the foil to vent his frustration. "And speaking of entertainment, the two couples were chatting with some other gawkers there about a show tomorrow night down at Kelly's. Some sort of art show with music or something. Like they weren't even standing around a murder scene."

"Hell," I said, "Elly and I are going to that show."

"Good, keep an eye on those sumbitches." He exhaled another loud breath of air. "Meantime, I'm gonna hit up on Judge Wilford again about a search warrant. I got a feeling a .22 caliber handgun might be around some place."

"That the murder weapon? A .22?"

"Can't be sure till the slugs are removed. But I bet that's

it." He muttered something I couldn't understand. Then he said, "And I'm checking more about that killing down in Florida, where two of those couples are from. See if they were in the area at that time."

I started to ask something else about the victim, Stafford, but Balls was through sounding off. He barked out, "Gotta go." And he was gone.

So, putting together what Balls said—and didn't say—I knew he was thinking that Stafford's killing and the couples were linked, the same as they were linked to the murders of the two young women.

I did too.

Chapter Sixteen

Late that afternoon Elly called from the courthouse. I glanced at my watch. It was time for her workday to have ended. She started right in: "I wanted to give you a ring before I left to go home. Early today I heard about the killing up at Duck."

News circulated rapidly in Dare County, and especially with the courthouse crowd.

She said, "Jarvis Stafford. I didn't know him personally, but I met him once or twice. He used to date a woman I know from Wanchese. Didn't he work up at that restaurant where you and Agent Twiddy had dinner?"

In the shortened version I had given her of the sessions Balls and I had in Duck, I eliminated any mention of talking with Stafford. And I wasn't sure how much I should say. But I went ahead and said, "Yeah, Balls and I chatted with him briefly at the restaurant. He was one of the chefs."

There was a pause, then, "Uh-oh."

"What do you mean, 'uh-oh'?"

"You and Agent Twiddy 'chat' with him and then he ends up getting himself killed." She sighed. "That's what I mean by uh-oh. It's all involved, isn't it? I mean the woman murdered and you check into that and then another person you've talked to ends up dead, too." Her voice had taken on an edge to it.

I tried to make my tone lighter. "You're beginning to

sound like Rick Schweikert." I attempted a short chuckle. Not sure it came across.

"I don't suppose you want to tell me whether there is a connection or not."

"Elly, I really don't know. I really don't. It does seem, well, curious though. And Balls is working on it. You can bank on that." I wanted to keep myself sounding as much like a bystander as possible.

She didn't say anything for a moment, and then when she did speak, her voice was softer, more relaxed. "Well, as I said last night I've accepted the fact that you're a crime writer, so I know you get . . . get involved from time to time." The trace of the Outer Banks hoigh-toide accent was there when she said "time to time." And I love to hear it.

Before she hung up and locked the office for the night, we agreed that I would pick her up at six-thirty tomorrow night for the show at Kelly's. I didn't mention that I expected the three couples to attend also.

It was the next afternoon, Friday, before I heard from Balls again. "Got the final report in from Chapel Hill. Autopsy on Sharon Dawson. Just like you figured, she was dead before she was trussed up. Heavily drugged." He named the drug that was used but I didn't catch it. "After she was out—and a little sex play was involved—she was smothered, probably with a pillow or something soft like that."

"Raped?"

"No, not raped. But before she was killed she may have been sexually active, as they say. Or someone may have been sexually active with her."

"DNA?"

"This ain't TV. The labs are so backed up on DNA testing might be July before we'd find out." He hesitated a moment. "But, tell you the truth, whoever did this was careful enough I don't think we'd find any DNA anyway."

"Any more on Stafford?"

"No." There was another pause.

"Judge still holding out on no search warrant?"

"Yep. They bend over backwards to keep from embarrassing any of the tour-eye."

He was quiet for so long that I said, "You still there?"

"Thinking," he said. I knew there was something else that prompted his call. "Listen, tonight at Kelly's, don't make it look like you're staking out those couples, if they do show up."

"I won't. I'll have Elly with me. May not even see them. Be a lot of folks there. But I guess I'll speak to them if I do see them. Okay?"

"Sure. Just act surprised that they're there, too."

"Got it," I said. To myself I thought that I didn't want to subject Elly to even meeting them, having her in the presence of a person or persons who might be killers.

Balls must have read my thoughts. "Might want to keep the Pedersen gal away from them."

We signed off and I took a shower; preparations to go get Elly. I wore the usual khakis, but a button-down oxford shirt, and even had socks on with my boat shoes.

I got to Elly's at six-fifteen. The late afternoon light cast long shadows across her yard from the pine trees that lined the road. I was a little early so she didn't appear on the porch. I tapped on the front door and Mrs. Pedersen appeared and invited me in with a smile. Martin stood a pace or two behind her, eyeing me.

"I'll be right out," Elly called from the back.

I settled on the sofa, checking out the crossword of that day. She had filled it all in. Martin stayed in the living room with me. I asked him how he was doing. He nodded. I caught him looking at me from time to time.

Mrs. Pedersen came back in the room. "Martin, why don't you show Mr. Weaver the drawing you did today?"

Without a word, he went down the hall and came back with a piece of notebook paper and showed it to me. "Hey, this is good, Martin," I said.

It was a colored pencil drawing of a beach and water, the sun in the sky, and two stick figures walking close together.

Mrs. Pedersen said, "He told me that's you and his mother on the beach."

"Oh, that's really sweet, Martin. May I have it? I can put it on my refrigerator with the other one you gave me."

He smiled. "Okay," he said softly.

Elly came out. She looked lovely. She wore trim, cream-colored slacks, flats, and a peach cotton blouse with her white cardigan sweater, unbuttoned. Her dark hair was brushed back from her face a bit. The light shined on her hair and in her eyes.

"Beautiful," I said.

"Thank you, kind sir. You look good yourself."

For probably the first time, Martin didn't start to tear up as we prepared to leave. I thanked him again for the drawing, and he nodded solemnly.

When we pulled into the parking lot at Kelly's shortly before seven, there were already a number of cars present. I saw a black SUV with Ohio tags, and thought that might be one of the couples, but I didn't say anything. We found a spot at the south side of the lot. I came around to open Elly's door, but she had already started out. "Sorry," she said. "I can't get used to being with a gentleman."

"Bull," I said.

She took my arm, and glanced up at the evening sky. It was clear and there was a light breeze coming from the southwest. A most pleasant late spring evening. We could smell the comfortable odor of food as we entered the heavy wooden door to Kelly's. "I'm already hungry," Elly said.

"For a little bitty girl you can put the food away," I said. "Never gain an ounce."

"I burn it off worrying about you," she said with a laugh, and squeezed my arm.

We were greeted by the hostess and told her we were going into the grill for the fund-raising show. Owner Mike

Kelly stood smiling near the door to the grill and we shook hands. Inside the door, Laura and others from the Dare County Arts Council were checking folks in. There was a large jar there for donations. I put in a couple of tens. The place was active and busy with people moving about and talking rather loudly. Surprisingly, we found a table for two next to the dance floor. Most of the tables were occupied by four, six or more people. The stage was empty except for the musicians' instruments. All of the amplifiers were in place. There were a couple of guitars, a set of drums, a keyboard and an upright bass lying on its side.

As I helped Elly into her seat, I glanced around discreetly to see if the three couples were present. Yes, they were. They were seated at a table at the far end of the dance floor. They appeared engrossed in talking with each other and obviously had not seen me. That was good. There'd be time to speak with them, if the occasion presented itself. After all, Balls didn't say *not* to speak to them. But if I did, I wanted to speak to them without Elly, if feasible. I sat with my back to the couples.

In a minute or so, a young waitress bustled over to our table and asked if we wanted drinks before we ordered. We both ordered sweetened ice tea. She hurried away. I looked around the area. Sitting at the bar was round-face Deputy Dorsey in civilian clothes. He nodded solemnly when our eyes met. Uh-huh, sent there by Balls, I was sure.

"Lot of people here," Elly said brightly, glancing around the large room, and up to the balcony where tables were beginning to be occupied.

When the waitress came back with the iced tea, we both ordered the coconut shrimp, and laughed that we were ordering the same thing. "We could order something different and then share," she said.

A short while later, Laura took the stage to welcome everyone for coming and for supporting the Arts Council. She said there would be three musical groups tonight—one in which her husband played drums, and Andy Rice played bass, and then the featured group from Ocracoke Island, Molasses Creek, plus Old Enough to Know Better. All three bands were great, I knew, and I especially liked hearing Marcy Brenner and Lou Castro with Molasses Creek. Someone from the audience shouted out to Laura, "Hey, Patsy, aren't you going to sing?"

Laura did a wonderful imitation of Patsy Cline, a show she had done before. "Okay," she said. "In a minute." Her husband's band came up on stage. Laura conferred with her husband, Dan. He counted off a rather slow tempo and the familiar strains of "Crazy" started and Laura took the microphone and began to sing. Perfect. Elly and I both leaned forward, listening and enjoying. I could hear Andy Rice doing an excellent job on the bass, giving a foundation for each note she sang. It made me want to start playing with a band again. I had put it off since moving to the Outer Banks. I wasn't sure I ever wanted to do it again, reminding me too much of the years I'd played, and Keely sang with various bands—until she began to sink deeper and deeper into depresssion, where no one could reach her. Then there was that day I found her and the empty pill bottles, and she was dead, curled up in the bed.

I realized Elly was watching my face. I shook that image of Keely out of my head, and smiled at Elly, coming back to the music on stage.

The waitress brought our coconut shrimp and we dived right in. The coleslaw was good and the French fries were done to perfection. Rolls and a couple of hushpuppies too.

The band played several more numbers. On one of them, "Sophisticated Lady," Andy Rice did an excellent solo around the melody. I said, "Wow," softly to Elly and shook my head in admiration. "He's good. Really good," I said. After one more song, Laura came back to the microphone to say there'd be a short intermission and then Molasses Creek would play.

I had almost forgotten about the three couples at the other end of the dance floor, when I felt a light tap on my shoulder. I turned around. It was Denis and Dewey Farrish, the D and D from Dayton. I stood and extended my hand. Denise smiled, rather wanly I thought. Her hand was limp. Dewey's handshake was not much firmer.

"Oh, Denise and Dewey," I said, "this is my dear friend Elly." Then, noticing they both wore light windbreakers, I said, "You're not leaving?"

"Yes," she said, "we're heading on back."

"All the way back," Dewey said dryly.

I raised an eyebrow and tilted my head.

"Yes," Denise said. "Maybe our caravan days are over."

I looked at Elly and said, "Will you excuse me a minute? I'll walk out with them."

Elly knew something was up. She smiled and said, "Certainly. Good to have met both of you."

They acknowledged her comment and turned to make their exit. I noticed out of the corner of my eye that Deputy Dorsey was watching us and had begun to move from the bar toward the exit. "Be right back," I whispered to Elly. She nodded. As I followed Denise and Dewey to the door for the grillroom, I saw that the other two couples watched us.

In the foyer, I stopped. They seemed eager to leave but they stopped also and turned toward me. "Don't mean to pry," I said, "but something the matter?"

"No, not really," Dewey said. "Nothing to talk about. Just doesn't seem like much fun anymore."

"Yes, that's it," Denise said.

I didn't believe either one of them. I knew there was more to it than that. But obviously they were not going to talk about it.

Dewey read the doubt in my face. So he said, with what he apparently hoped would be further clarification, "I guess they're just younger than we are. Have different interests."

"Yes, that's it," Denise agreed. "Different interests." They made their way toward the front doors.

"Just a minute," I said, and retrieved a business card from my wallet. "Here's my card. Call me if you want to talk about anything . . . anything at all."

He looked at me as if he might say something else. But he just nodded, acknowledging what I had said. She wouldn't meet my gaze.

"Well, good to see both of you," I said, trying to make it sound casual.

I turned to go back in the grillroom. Dorsey stood at the doorway. I said, "Call Balls and tell him the couple from Dayton have left the others . . . left in sort of a tiff."

"A tiff?"

"Yes. Upset. They're a little upset by something. They say they're leaving the caravan."

"Caravan?"

"Tell him they're leaving the caravan, and they're upset about something." He'll understand."

"Yes, sir."

"Thanks, Dorsey." I touched his muscular shoulder and grinned. "You don't have to sir me."

"Yes . . ." He nodded, and pulled a cell phone from his belt. "I'll call him right now. See if he wants me to follow them."

"I doubt it," I said. "I'm going back in."

"Oh, Mr. Weaver?"

"Yes?" I could hear the band starting up.

"Elly Pedersen is a nice lady—and real pretty, too."

I stopped. "Yes, she is," I said. "I'll tell her you said so."

Dorsey's round boyish face actually flushed a bit.

Molasses Creek band was really rocking when I stepped back into the grillroom and made my way to Elly and our table. Marcy Brenner was singing a duet with one of the other band members close to the standup microphone, but I couldn't make out lyrics, except that they were exuberant and joyful.

The other two couples ignored me as I came back into the room, concentrating on watching the band. At least they appeared to be ignoring me. I took my seat at our small table. "Sorry," I said, "but I needed to check with them." I had to lean forward toward her as I spoke because the music was loud.

"They're part of that group from the mountains, aren't they?" I watched her lips as she spoke, partly to understand what she was saying and partly because I liked to watch the way her lips moved when she talked.

I nodded.

She smiled and reached across the table and touched my hand. "You'll tell me when you can tell me." Then she put on a mock conspiratorial expression. "The other two couples they were with are still back there. They look at us from time to time."

I stared into her eyes. "Thanks, Elly. Didn't know you had noticed." Then, smiling brightly, I leaned toward her and told her what Deputy Dorsey had said.

"That was sweet," she said.

Before the next number started, our waitress appeared and asked about dessert. "Why not?" I said. Elly ordered a *crème brulé* and I got the chocolate mousse.

Marcy and her husband Lou Castro were engaged in a duet in the next number when the waitress returned with our desserts. The band's music was hard to define—maybe a cross between country western, Cajun, and bluegrass. But it was lively and certainly toe-tapping and the audience applauded enthusiastically.

Old Enough to Know Better came on next, a swinging group with an excellent vocalist, Betsy Robinson, plus a great electric bass player and drummer.

By close to nine the show was winding down. People had begun to leave. Laura announced there'd be one more number.

Elly appeared to be watching the band, but she said to me, "They're leaving. Coming this way."

I had just risen to speak to Jim, a friend and neighbor, when the other two couples approached. They had to pass our table on the way out. I turned to them as they paused to speak. Stan and Becky were in front. "Well, where's your sidekick?" Stan said, a smirk rather than a smile on his face.

Looking as pleasant as I could, I said, "You mean SBI Agent Twiddy? Oh, I'm sure he's out making America safe for you and me."

Stan's wife smiled her brittle smile, and Karl and Velda came up and spoke. "We keeping running into you," Velda said, sounding languid and relaxed.

"It's really a small sandbar," I said.

Karl smiled and tilted his head toward the band. "Good show," he said.

As they made their way toward the exit I saw Dorsey watching. I held my hand to the side of my head like a cell phone, and he nodded.

"Sorry I didn't introduce you," I said to Elly.

"Just as well," she said. "Don't need to mix business and pleasure." She gave a short laugh. "Not sure that came out the way I intended."

I handed my credit card to the waitress. When she came back and I had signed the slip, I suggested to Elly that we speak to Lou Castro and Marcy and thank them for their performance. I also ran into Andy Rice, the bass player, and complimented him. As we left, we told Laura it was a great show.

When we stepped outside and breathed in the mild night air coming off the ocean, I said, "Well, it's all pleasure now. No business."

"Still rather early," she said.

"Yes?" Then a pause because I wasn't sure what to propose.

"Harrison, let's go to your house."

I looked at her. I'm sure a bit of shock registered on my face.

"Yes," she said, and lifted her chin in a gesture that was part defiance and part resolution, "I've been thinking about it."

"A pleasure," I said.

Chapter Seventeen

As we drove up the Bypass, Elly sat quietly beside me, lost in thought. Maybe I was too. I was a little nervous, I realized. I knew that suggesting we come to my house was not simply a casual thought. The next level? I was sure that it was.

We pulled into my cul-de-sac, still talking very little. I was glad the carport light was on and a lamp glowed in the window upstairs in the living room.

"Looks right homey, Harrison," she said. The word "right" came out with that soft Outer Banks accent.

I thought about the fact that, except for the bass lying on the living room floor, and maybe a few of Janey's seeds she'd tossed about, the place was neat and clean. Even the dinette table, with my laptop and papers on it, was orderly. Admittedly, I'm a bit fussy about keeping the place picked up. Bed made, too, and relatively fresh sheets on it.

We went up the outside stairs that lead to the kitchen door. As we went inside there was the slightest aroma of coffee, probably from the grinder. "It's nice, Harrison. Like I remember it."

She had only been here once before, almost a year ago. We had sat on the sofa and gone into an embrace that promised to develop further when I got a telephone call I couldn't ignore—and the spell was broken. She left shortly after that.

"I've got some iced tea, coffee, and that's about it," I said.

"I'd love a glass of water," she said. She took off her cardigan sweater and laid it across the back of one of the easy chairs.

As I fixed her water with a couple of cubes of ice in it, and poured myself a tumbler of iced tea, she stepped over the neck of the bass and spoke to Janey, who ignored her completely. Speaking to Janey, Elly said, "You still saying those naughty words, little bird?"

"Once in a while," I chuckled, and walked over to where she stood and handed her the water. Janey began to do her head-bopping as I came to her cage. When Elly was here before, she swore that Janey said the word "bitch." But I told her that female parakeets didn't talk. That was a lie, of course, because Janey, after spending hours listening to me practice the bass and fuss about Mozart and others, had picked up the words "bitch" and "shit."

Elly took a long sip of her water and then sat on the sofa, putting her glass on one of the coasters on the coffee table. When I'd moved in, I had bought rattan furniture in light colors that seemed to reflect the beach and sunshine. She looked around the room, smiling. "You're doing well," she said.

I came over and sat beside her. Yes, I could feel my heart beating faster. I tried to act casual, but it was difficult for me to do.

She took another sip of her water.

"Okay, Harrison," she said. "I've got my little speech all prepared."

I watched her lips and eyes, not at all sure what was coming next. Her face was pleasant, though, a look of almost serenity glowed.

She removed her right hand from the water glass and clasped her hands in her lap, staring straight at me. "I'm an Outer Banks girl—woman—and probably because of that I think I'm tough and straightforward. And I've been thinking about us and how we've grown closer and closer, and how both of us—not just me—have backed away from time to time, and usually right at the moment when things could, well, go farther." She took a deep breath, and reached one hand out and rested it gently on my forearm. "I'm here tonight, Harrison, to tell you that I'm not backing away any longer. I've made up my mind . . . and I guess I'm in love with you . . . and . . ."

She couldn't finish because I put my arm around her, pulled her to me and kissed those lips, and the kiss grew and she opened her mouth and I felt her tongue.

When we finally broke the kiss, our eyes boring into each other, I whispered, "And I love you, Elly . . . and I don't say that lightly."

"I know," she said.

Then she stood and took my hand and I stood with her and without speaking we moved into the bedroom.

I stood there watching her as she began to take off her golf shirt. I was nervous and I stared at her, fascinated. She folded her blouse loosely and laid it carefully across the back of a chair. Her bra was off-white. She kicked off her flats and undid the top of her slacks. I began to undress also. We still hadn't spoken but she kept the slight, almost enigmatic smile on her lips. I removed my shirt, and bent over rather awkwardly and took off my socks and boat shoes.

Her slacks came off and she carefully laid those on the chair. She stood there in her bra and low-rise pale blue cotton panties. She looked lovely. I took off my slacks and shorts in one movement. I was excited, and I felt my heart beating.

She looked at me and said, "Oh, my." And she smiled.

She undid her bra and then stepped out of her panties.

"You are beautiful," I said. "Absolutely beautiful."

"Well, I'm natural, anyway," she said.

"I love it," I said.

We embraced and she said again, "Oh, my."

I pulled back the bedspread and was glad again that the

sheets were fresh. We lay down, facing each other. Her breasts were larger than I thought they would be and I began to kiss her. I could hear her breathing and the quickening of her breath as I kissed her and I loved that.

Then I looked up at her and said, "I don't have any . . . any . . ."

She smiled at me and put her hand on the top of my head. "From what I've read, this is a safe time of month for me," she said, and managed a little laugh that, though tinged with nervousness, came across as loving.

I kept on kissing her breasts, and then her stomach and she couldn't keep still. She made little noises in her throat.

In a little while I came up to her and she guided me, and she said again, "Oh, my."

Afterwards, we lay there together, smiling at each other. She said, "So this is what it's all about. Just like the storybooks and the movies have said." Then she gave another of her little laughs. "They weren't kidding."

"Wonderful," I said.

"But aren't we both supposed to be here smoking cigarettes now?"

"I've got a cigar or two," I said. "We could light those."

"Not the same."

I put my hand down her stomach. "I love touching you," I said.

"All natural," she said.

"Like crisp, fresh parsley."

She laughed. "Yes, you *are* a writer."

Later, when we were redressed and she looked at the clock over the kitchen sink, she said, "I guess you'd better . . ."

"I know," I said. "We don't want your mother to think we've completely disappeared."

She smiled. "I told her it might be late when I got home."

"You had this planned, didn't you?"

She picked up her sweater from the back of the chair. "I told you I'd been thinking."

"And being an Outer Banks gal . . ."

"That's right."

Driving back home after I had taken Elly to Manteo, I took
the Bypass and stayed slightly below the speed limit, thinking. I felt loving and good but at the same time perhaps just a
little bit afraid. Elly and I had turned a significant corner. I
realized that, yes, we are a couple now. We've acted like a
dating couple; now it was different. Maybe we'd have a certain glow about us that people could see. I smiled to myself
and pulled into my cul-de-sac and parked. I turned the ignition off but sat there in the car a minute or two. Then I went
upstairs, spoke to Janey, and suddenly had that urge for
another cigar. I got a cigar and started to the sliding doors
that led out to the deck when I noticed the message light
blinking on my answering machine. It was now after eleven-
thirty. I hesitated and then punched the playback button.

The voice was a little breathless, a touch of anxiety in
the tone: "Mr. Weaver, this is Denise Farrish. I know it's late
but Dewey and I've been talking and, well, maybe there *is*
something else we need to talk with you about. I mean about
our leaving the caravan and all. Probably nothing but we
thought, well, we thought maybe we should say something."
It sounded like she momentarily put her hand over the
mouthpiece, probably conferring with Dewey, and then she
came back on: "Maybe tomorrow, before we leave, we could
meet there at that Market Place shopping center. We'll be on
our way north. Dewey says there's a bagel shop there.
Bonnie's Bagels. We'll stop there about nine-thirty or ten,
and if you get this message and want to meet us . . . well,
we'll be there."

The message ended.

I wanted to call Balls. This could really be significant. I
glanced at my watch again, knowing what time it was, and
decided I'd wait until first thing in the morning, early. I
knew I couldn't sleep now, so I went out on the deck and lit

my cigar.

What a night, I thought. What a night.

Chapter Eighteen

I slept fitfully, and waked completely by five-thirty. Just before six I dialed Balls' cell phone. After a couple of rings I didn't think he would answer. Then I heard a gruff, "Yeah?"

I told him about the message I'd received from Denise Farrish.

"Shit," he said. "I've got to be in Elizabeth City for a meeting at nine-thirty." He was silent a moment, then he said, "Come to think of it, though, it may be best if you are there by yourself. I might spook them. She'll probably talk to you easier than she would to me. Just make sure you remember everything she says—and doesn't say." He chuckled. "Little old ladies seem to like you anyway for some God-knows reason."

"It's because I'm a shy, sensitive, retiring type," I said.

"Yeah, and full of crap." He got serious again. "I have a feeling the Farrish lady might help us narrow this thing down a bit. Frankly, I'm zeroing in on the other two couples anyway. Something dirty about them."

"Both couples?"

"I don't know, yet. But I got a feeling we're getting closer. We know there was a similar killing in Florida. Still unsolved."

"Anywhere else?"

"Not that I know of yet." Another pause at his end. "Be sure to get back with me just as soon as you meet with the

Farrish couple."

"I will."

Before we signed off he said, "Oh, Deputy Dorsey kept me informed last night—especially how you were squiring that Pedersen gal around."

"We were having dinner and listening to the bands," I said.

"Yeah, sure," he said.

The hours dragged that morning. I was dressed and ready to go to Bonnie's Bagels by eight-thirty. I kept checking my watch. I called Elly at work. At first she sounded a bit businesslike. Then I could tell she got more privacy from her coworkers. She said softly, a trace of laughter in her voice, "You still respect me after last night."

I chuckled too. "Even more so, you wild kid, you."

Then I told her about the call last night and where I was going. I told her that Balls would not be there. She was silent a moment, then said, "I believe you're going to find out something most interesting."

"I hope so. We could use a break in this."

"There's that 'we' business again."

"Well, you know."

"Yeah, yeah."

I heard her coworkers in the background. She got matter-of-fact again and said, "Call me when you get through with your appointment." We signed off.

A couple of minutes after nine I got in my Subaru and drove up to Mile Post 1 and the Market Place shopping center. The sun was out and it was balmy and warm. I parked close by Bonnie's, down below CVS drugstore, and looked around at the other vehicles. A couple of sedans, a white SUV, and a pickup truck. No one occupied the wicker chairs and table out front. I went in, spoke to Star, the young woman working there, and ordered a plain bagel, lightly toasted with a light spread of strawberry cream cheese, a small Italian coffee, which wasn't really all that small. I got my coffee and told Star I would take it outside. She volunteered to bring the bagel to me.

I took a seat in one of the chairs at the table just outside the front door. I had a good view of any traffic coming and going. I checked the time again. Just nine-eighteen. In a few minutes Star brought my bagel and spoke a moment about what a nice day it was.

I ate slowly. Before coming I had thought about bringing my small tape recorder but figured that would not be a good idea as nervous as Denise Farrish had sounded. I did have my usual reporter's notebook in the back pocket of my khakis, but I was not at all sure I would even use that. I didn't want to risk having Denise or Dewey not feeling free to talk. I knew I could remember everything they said.

At nine thirty-five they still hadn't come. I sipped my coffee. Nine forty-five, no sign of them. Then, just a minute or two before ten, I saw them pull up in a Dodge Journey SUV and park in one of the handicapped places. Dewey drove and Denise handed him a placard that he hung on the review mirror. They got out rather slowly, and I noticed for the first time that Dewey favored his left leg considerably. They saw me. I stood as they approached. He didn't smile and she managed just a trace of a greeting. I shook hands with both of them and tried to act very casual and friendly.

"Can I get you something?" I said.

"I'll go in and get it," he said. "Thanks anyway," he mumbled.

I waited until Denise sat and then I took my chair again.

"I see you got my message," she said. She fumbled with her pocketbook, putting it first in her lap, then on the table, then back on her lap again.

"I appreciate your call," I said.

"Well, I don't know . . ." Her voice trailed off. "Maybe I shouldn't have called and left that message . . ." Again she hesitated, let her voice drop so that it was almost inaudible.

I figured I'd try to put her more at ease. "Sorry you all are leaving. The weather is getting really nice now. Wonderful time, late spring, here at the Outer Banks." I smiled brightly.

"Yes, it's pretty," she said but didn't sound as if she had noticed the weather.

Dewey pushed open the door, carrying two coffees. "The girl will bring a couple of bagels," he said. He hadn't smiled yet. He took his seat, stared at me a moment, then said, "Now, Mr. Weaver, I want you to know—we both want you to know—that whatever we say is confidential. And probably not worth anything at all anyway."

Denise spoke up, "Too, we feel a little, well, we feel a little disloyal for even suggesting that we talk to you."

"That's true," Dewey said.

"I can assure you," I said, "that you can speak to me in confidence." I didn't tell them that I'd run right to Balls with anything they told me.

She spoke again: "We figured that as a writer, interested in this whole business, that you'd be better to talk to, you know, unofficially, instead of talking to that SBI friend of yours."

"Yes," Dewey said. "You can weigh what we say—and either forget it, figuring our imagination has run away with us, or not."

"Please," I said, and I tried to look as sincere and understanding as possible. "Please feel free to talk with me openly and freely. Let's just sit here with our coffee and bagels and chat."

At just that moment Star came out with two cinnamon burst bagels, thick with cream cheese. They smelled good. I took the last tiny bite of my bagel, and a sip of my now lukewarm coffee. "Thanks, Star," I said. She hurried back inside.

Denise looked at me. "You must come here often."

I smiled and nodded.

Dewey took a mouthful of bagel and wiped cream cheese off his lower lip with one of the paper napkins Star had brought.

"I know you're wondering why we're leaving our little

caravan," Denise said.

"We just don't think we fit in anymore," Dewey said, chewing, and speaking with a goodly portion of the bagel still in his mouth.

"They're a lot younger than we are, for one thing," Denise said.

Okay, I thought. Enough preliminary chitchat. "But that's not the only reason, is it?" I stared at both of them in turn, looking serious.

Dewey put down his bagel. "No, it's not."

Denise said, "There are some things that probably you don't know . . ."

Dewey spoke sharply to his wife. "You want to do the talking or me?"

"You," she said quietly, picking at her bagel.

"Well, both of us," he said. I assumed it was his way of apologizing. Nothing was said for a moment and then Dewey spoke to Denise. "You started to say—"

She looked up at me. "That night I first saw you at the restaurant up in Duck, and I thought I recognized you. Well, the other two couples—Stan and Becky and Karl and Velda—well, they didn't let on at the time, but they had seen you and recognized you earlier."

I know I wrinkled my brow, not grasping what she was saying.

"Maybe four or five days earlier at that art show, the one at Ghost Ship Gallery, or something."

"Ghost Fleet Gallery," I said, remembering going there the Friday night before my aborted kayak outing that Saturday morning. There was a large crowd for an opening of the Frank Stick Memorial Art Show. "I didn't see them," I said.

"Yeah, but they saw you," Dewey said. "They admitted that to us that second night at the restaurant after you and Agent Twiford left us."

"Agent Twiddy," I said softly.

"After you two left, they said they'd seen you there and

you were talking with some friends, talking about kayaking or something."

I remembered that, too, and a little bell began to ring in the back of my mind. "Yes," I said. "Several of my friends who are into kayaking and biking were there."

"Then that first night on the porch at the restaurant, I thought I recognized you, and I mentioned it but they didn't say anything then. I don't know why," she said.

I watched both of them intently. I knew there was more they needed and wanted to say. I figured I'd try to move them forward a bit. "The fact that they recognized me—recognized me from when I was up at Mattaskeet—and didn't say anything is curious, but that's about all . . . curious. It doesn't tell me much about why you're leaving, leaving your caravan, as you call it."

Dewey carefully tore off a piece of his bagel. He wiped a glob of the cream cheese from his index finger, put it back on the bagel, and brought it to his mouth, chewing slowly. Denise stared at her coffee. Then she looked up at me. "They were real friendly, real friendly, with the waitress there at Mattaskeet," she said. She thrust her chin forward. "In fact, you'd say they flirted with her. And she flirted back."

Dewey kept chewing, but he looked at me and nodded.

Denise continued. "Same with the waitress here at the Outer Banks." She shook her head. "Of course, we didn't know that was the young woman they found over wherever it was dead until you and, and, that detective told us it was the same person."

"They left really big tips," Dewey said. "Every time. Up at Mattaskeet and here. More than anyone would think about leaving. And I'm in the restaurant business."

I didn't say anything. It was obvious they believed or suspected that the other two couples knew more about the two murdered women than just seeing them at the restaurants. Okay, I thought, enough of this dancing around; so I said, "Do you think they had more contact with the two women than just there at each of the restaurants?"

Denise started to speak but Dewey interjected quickly, "Now, no we didn't say that. Didn't say that exactly." He shook his head. "No, that'd sound like we were accusing them, or something. We don't mean that . . . not exactly."

"What, then, *do* you believe?" I stared from one to the other. Neither one would meet my eyes.

Denise appeared on the verge of tears. "We're just, just uncomfortable," she said. There was a catch in her voice. "We just have a feeling, a feeling that makes us uncomfortable."

Dewey pushed the little tray with the last bite of his bagel away from him. "That's it. That's it exactly. We're uncomfortable being with them anymore—at least for now."

"We want to go home," Denise said.

The three of us sat there without speaking for a moment or two. A man and woman came toward the bagel shop. "Lovely day, isn't it?" the man said, and we smiled at them and agreed. They went inside.

"Now, as you know," I said, "I'm not an investigator. I'm a writer, that's all. But from what you're saying—and not saying—I have to believe that you think perhaps the other two couples—Stan and Becky, Karl and Velda—know more about these two women than . . . than makes you comfortable."

Dewey spoke quickly: "We're not accusing them. You understand that. We're not accusing them at all."

I kept quiet, waiting.

Denise took a sip of her coffee, put it down and began to clear her tray away, crumpling her napkin and depositing it in the tray, signaling that she was through. "I need to go to the restroom before we leave," she said to Dewey. He nodded. She went inside.

Dewey said, "I think my wife is a little more—more uncomfortable with being around Stan and Karl and their wives than I am." He tried to smile, and almost made it.

When Denise came back, we stood. It was obvious our little conversation was about over. Then Denise, fidgeting again with her pocketbook, turned to face me. "There's another thing that bothers me, bothers us," she said. "The other night when we were getting ready to leave the restaurant up at Duck, the night you and that other man talked with us, just as we were getting ready to leave that chef came out and asked us if we enjoyed the meal. He'd never come out and spoken before. We ate there a lot this week. And it was the way he looked at us. It wasn't real friendly, I didn't think. And then he ends up dead, too."

Dewey took his wife's elbow, preparing to guide her toward their vehicle. Again, he tried to bring forth a smile. "It's like everybody we come in contact with ends up dead."

"We're just not comfortable," Denise said. "Not comfortable at all."

I walked with them toward their Dodge SUV. A few feet from the car, Dewey stopped. He still held to Denise's elbow. "One other thing, Mr. Weaver," he said. "When our so-called caravan was on the way to the Outer Banks, and everywhere else, we always made a lot of stops along the way. Our way of enjoying the areas we visit, taking little side roads and bypaths, exploring. And it probably doesn't mean anything at all, but when we got close to the Outer Banks, we took that road off the highway that leads down to Buffalo City."

I felt a chill run down my spine.

"Where that poor woman was found," Denise said.

As if she had to remind me of it.

Chapter Nineteen

I watched them leave the Market Place shopping center and turn right on the Bypass, heading north.

I went back to the table in front of Bonnie's. I sat there trying to digest what Dewey and Denise Farrish had said, and what they had left unsaid. I wanted to gather my thoughts for a few minutes before I called Balls.

I went inside and got another cup of coffee, brought it outside to the table. I took a sip and then called Balls on my cell.

He answered on the third ring. He spoke quietly. "This better be good," he said. "Just stepped outside the meeting to take this call and I could use something good."

"Not sure," I said, "but here's what I got. Incidentally, they just left, heading back north."

"That's okay. I know where they live if I need them again."

"They never came out and accused the other two couples of anything. In fact, they kept denying they were accusing them. Just the same, I know they suspect something. They kept saying they were uncomfortable being around them any longer. They did say the others were overly friendly—flirty—with both waitresses . . . the one at Mattaskeet and this one here."

"Sharon Dawson."

"Yeah. And too, the other two couples had seen me

earlier at Ghost Fleet Gallery and hadn't mentioned anything about it to Dewey and Denise Farrish."

Balls made a puzzled "hmm" sound.

"And the other two couples had heard me talking about kayaking. I didn't see them. Then as the Farrish couple were leaving a few minutes ago, they also said that as part of their exploring along the way to different places they had driven into Buffalo City."

"Now that *is* interesting," Balls said. "Maybe, as I've said, a message . . . to you."

"Doesn't sound as farfetched as it did when you first mentioned it."

"It's not." He gave a chuckle that sounded more like a snort. "I mean we're dealing with a really weird killer or killers, and they can get kicks different ways."

"Another thing they told me, and made a point of telling me, was that the chef, Jarvis Stafford, came up to their table that night after you and I left and spoke to them. Asked if they'd enjoyed the meal, but Denise said he didn't really seem all that friendly." I paused a moment. "You remember he was watching us that night as we left."

Balls was quiet. I waited. Then he said, "There's a connection. With the Stafford guy's killing. And I think we both know what it is."

I hoped he would say more. He didn't, so I said, "Reward?"

"More like extortion. At least attempted and botched extortion." Then he said, "I gotta get back in there. Anything else—for now?"

"It occurred to me, but I've more or less dismissed it, do you think the Farrish couple is trying to throw suspicion onto the others, when they're the ones actually involved?"

It was a real chuckle this time. "You're getting jaded and suspicious, which can be good, but in this case, I can't quite see that little old lady and her husband doing in young women, and getting them naked, either before or after they kill them, then carting them off somewhere."

"I have a hard time imaging anybody doing that," I said, even though I've come to realize that human beings can do all manner of unimaginable things to one another.

When I put the cell phone away, I thought again about the difficulty Balls was having in getting a search warrant. Jeeze, the fact that Stafford got three bullets in him and he had at least some contact with the three couples, that ought to be enough to have that judge issue a search warrant, look for a small caliber handgun if nothing else. I wondered if Balls would be pushing the judge on that anymore today. Well, it *was* his investigation, I reminded myself, not mine.

Then I remembered I'd promised to call Elly.

"How has your morning gone?" she asked, a lilt to her voice and I knew that was code, so to speak, for the fact that her coworkers were nearby.

I gave her a much-shortened version of my meeting with the Farrish couple, mostly giving their reason for leaving as being "uncomfortable."

"More to it than that?" she said, the cheery tone still there.

"Probably," I said.

"I understand." Then she said, "On a totally different topic, how'd you like to go with me to the Dare County Arts Council's reception and show tonight? I know it's two nights in a row with an Arts Council function, but it *is* their special weekend—and Linda Shackleford's younger sister, Laura, is all excited because she's had three paintings accepted for the show."

"Be delighted," I said.

Then quietly, almost a whisper, Elly said, "I know Linda is pleased that Laura is showing an interest in something besides men."

I knew that about Laura, also, the business about an interest in men. She was as "fun-loving," to use that expression again, as her older sister Linda was conservative.

"Pick you up about six-thirty, grab a bite somewhere?"

"Fine, but plan to have something with us. Mother will

have fixed something."

We agreed. I needed to get back to the house, at least pretend to do a bit of work. But I couldn't help but think about the other two couples and wonder what they were doing. I wondered, too, what Balls would be up to. I knew he had a pressing investigation going on over in Elizabeth City—the slaying of an off-duty deputy sheriff. Killing of a law enforcement officer, off-duty or not, always received high priority. But I knew, too, that Balls was eager to get back onto these hogtieing killings—and the shooting of Jarvis Stafford.

After a light but tasty spring supper at Elly's we drove into downtown Manteo to attend the art show. We found a place to park on Budleigh Street, a few doors from the Pioneer Theater. To refer to Manteo's "downtown" is not as much of a stretch as it used to be. The county seat of Dare County, it has changed quite a bit in the past few years. Certainly more of an artsy feel to the town, more cafes, coffee shops, and galleries. And across the waterfront at Roanoke Island Festival Park, there's a replica of the Queen Elizabeth II, the type of sailing vessel that brought the ill-fated "lost colony" to the Outer Banks in 1587. At Festival Park there's a large orchestra shell for outdoor concerts, a gift shop and museum. It has become quite an attraction for tourists and residents alike.

Elly and I strolled into the art show, which already bustled with people. A volunteer stood behind a small table with tiny plastic wine glasses with punch. I noticed that white and red wines were also available. We spotted a couple of the artists we knew. We spoke to local artist and illustrator James Melvin. A year earlier I had purchased one of his prints of a beach house porch with a view of the ocean. His paintings always have an air of peace about them.

Elly kept looking around for Laura Shackleford. We saw her sister, Linda, first. She hurried over to us, a big toothy smile on her face. I've always sensed that Linda could bite through rawhide with those teeth. She had a camera slung around her neck. She gave Elly a quick hug and said to me, "How you doing, Scoop?"

"You're the reporter now, not me," I said.

"Good turnout," Elly said, stepping back to let a couple pass by us.

"Oh, it's great," Linda said.

"Where's Laura?" Elly glanced toward the adjoining areas of the main room where we stood. We moved again to let others get past us.

"Right around the corner," Linda said. "In that little alcove." She leaned in closer to us, that smile even bigger. "Two couples are in there admiring her paintings, and I think she may be about ready to sell one or two of them. Oh, that would be great. A big boost for her."

Although sisters, Linda and Laura couldn't be less alike. Linda was a good eleven years older than Laura, and big boned and husky, whereas Laura was petite and actually much prettier. If I had to class them as animals, which I have a habit of doing, I'd describe Laura as a frisky fawn and Linda as, well, as a sturdy ox. But I liked Linda a lot. She was solid, and a faithful friend of Elly's.

"We'll step around so we can peep in," Elly said, "but we won't go in just yet and distract her."

But at just that moment, Laura scurried around the corner toward us, a slip of paper in her hand. She saw us and paused midstride long enough to whisper, "I just sold this one, full price, and they may buy another one!" She took the slip of paper to another of the volunteers at a makeshift table and area that served as cashier. Then Laura hurried back around the corner.

Linda grinned proudly. "That's my baby sister. Good going."

We began to move around, looking at the art and sidestepping other viewers. Some of the art was quite good. Lot of sea scenes, naturally, and lighthouses dominate in quite a few. But the works included everything from abstracts to impressionism.

Turning one of the corners, we could catch a view into the alcove where Laura had her art. Another artist was in there, also, talking to two women who inspected her work. Laura stood facing us, smiling at two couples that had their backs to us. We tried not to be too obvious about watching to see what was going on. Laura smiled broadly and said something to one of the men, then proudly affixed a "sold" sign on the second of her pictures. We couldn't help but enjoy the glow on her face, happy for her. Her pictures, both of them beach scenes in early morning, were done in acrylic. They were adequate; not stunning.

Just then one of the foursome turned slightly. I felt a chill down my spine, an actual chill.

"What's the matter?" Elly said, touching my arm.

"It's them," I whispered. "It's the two couples."

We stepped back around the edge of the alcove, out of Laura's line of vision.

"You mean . . . you mean the couples that . . ."

I nodded. "Yes."

"Oh, my," Elly said.

I knew she studied my face. "You going to talk to them?" she said.

"Yes." I took a deep breath and we stepped around the corner into the alcove. The two women continued engaged with the other artist. Laura smiled and laughed at something one of the couples said.

I stepped forward. "Well," I said, "it seems we run into each other at every turn."

Karl extended his hand. "Once again," he said, and swept those sleepy eyes around the alcove and beyond. "Quite a show," he said.

"Yes," Velda said, her head held languidly to the side. "And we've just found a wonderful artist and love her work." She tilted her chin toward a beaming Laura.

I introduced Elly, who managed a rather brave smile.

Stan glanced around. "Where's your sidekick?"

My voice level, my eyes right on Stan, I said, "If you mean Agent Twiddy, he's got other duties to perform."

"No offense," Stan said.

His wife kept that brittle smile on her face. She appeared to appraise Elly, who looked ill at ease, her hands clutched together in front of her.

I figured I'd wade right in. "Had coffee and a bagel with Dewey and Denise this morning, just before they left headed north."

"Yeah," Stan said. "They decided to leave our little caravan."

"I wondered why," I said, letting my eyes sweep to each of them.

Karl smiled pleasantly. "I think our travels had gone on long enough for them . . . this time."

"They're a bit older than we are," Stan's wife said. "I think they were just tired."

"And we don't always travel together, matter of fact," Stan said.

His wife spoke again. "Yes, last spring Stan and I went to Colorado. I think Denise and Dewey went to some godforsaken place in Ohio or Indiana or somewhere . . ."

Velda spoke up, "And Karl and I went to Paris. Paris, France."

"Ah, Paris in April," old sleepy-eyes Karl said.

"I don't like Paris," Stan's wife said. "Too old, too dirty, too noisy, too many people."

Velda shrugged. "I love it. It's exciting."

Karl smiled at her.

Then Velda spoke to Elly. "You from here?"

"Yes," Elly said. "A native. Outer Banks native."

"Not too many of those around," Karl said, the smile still there.

"I'm a native, too," Laura said.

"You do beautiful work," Stan's wife said. Then she added, "We'd like to get to know you better, how you got started, where you studied.

"Oh, I'm self-taught," Laura said. She squirmed with pleasure.

"Really? Amazing," Velda said.

Stan said, "Let's look around at the whole show." He smiled at Laura.

To Laura, Karl said, "Now we'll pick those pictures up shortly." He chuckled. "And don't you let anything happen to them—and don't resell them."

Laura stepped forward and shook Karl's hand. "Oh, they'll be right here for you," she said.

Stan and the others nodded at me and moved out of the alcove.

"Isn't this great?" Laura whispered.

"Wonderful," Elly said.

I wanted to say something to Laura, to caution her, tell her I didn't trust those two couples. Too, I didn't like they way they came on to her. But I couldn't say anything, I didn't think, not at this stage. Maybe a word to Linda. "We'll walk around a bit," I said. "And congratulations, Laura."

"Oh, yes, thank you. I'm so pleased."

I wanted to find Linda. I saw the flash of her camera, and we turned a corner. She took a picture of an artist standing near one of her paintings with three visitors looking on. After Linda jotted down names in her notepad, I approached her, Elly beside me. "Let me speak to you just a minute, Linda," I said.

"Sure, Scoop," she said, flashing those strong white teeth.

Elly pretended to study a watercolor of the Manteo waterfront while Linda and I stepped aside a pace or two.

I wasn't sure how much to say to Linda but I felt compelled to get her to deliver a warning, or a caution, to her sister Laura, who seemed so thrilled with the attention from the two couples the she couldn't keep still.

Linda saw the expression on my face. "Yeah, Weav, what is it? Something the matter?"

"Linda, please keep this to yourself, but I'm concerned about the couples who bought Laura's artwork."

"Their checks no good?"

"No, it's more than that." I took a deep breath. "I'm more than a little bit suspicious that the couples—or the men, or just one of them—may be in some way connected with the killing of Sharon Dawson. You know, Buffalo City. Maybe with another murder up in the mountains."

"Jesus, Weav." She looked around like she thought we might be jumped. She leaned in closer, whispering. "That's scary. Right here in the gallery."

"They're being real friendly with Laura, saying things like they'd like to get to know her better." I put my face even closer to Linda's, looking directly into her eyes. "Don't let Laura be taken in by them. Don't let her go off with them."

Linda puffed out a breath, blowing upwards a strand of hair that had fallen across her forehead. "Fat chance she'll listen to me. She never has in the past."

"But be careful how you say it. I don't want to have any talk going around about these people being under suspicion." I put my hand on Linda's shoulder. "Balls would . . . Agent Twiddy would probably hit me in the head for even saying this much to you, but I really think Laura needs to . . . to distance herself from these people. Maybe I'm being too cautious, but I saw the way they were playing up to Laura, and how much she was eating it up."

Linda said, "I'll go in and try to get her to cool it, maybe even go home early." She shook her head. "But I'll be surprised if she listens to me."

"I know," I said.

I rejoined Elly at the watercolor. She turned her head slightly. "Any luck?"

"Not sure. I was trying to get Linda to caution her sister."

Elly nodded. "I wish her luck."

"Yes."

In another section of the gallery, I saw the couple strolling casually around inspecting the art, making a comment every now and then.

Elly and I approached them. "Hope you are enjoying the show. A lot of talent," I said.

They spoke and smiled. Then Velda looked at Elly again, and back to me. "Is Elly your wife?"

This threw me off momentarily. Another emotion was there, too. I didn't like for them to even be looking at Elly. "I haven't been able to talk her into it yet," I said.

Elly linked her arm in mine and managed a smile; not one of her better ones.

Velda, her head tilted to the side in that lazy pose of hers, said, "I don't think you'll give up."

"No, I won't," I said.

Then her husband, Karl, said, "We'd better get back and pick up our artwork." To the others he said, "Late dinner? Lone Cedar or Tale of the Whale? I've been wanting to try those places out."

I watched them move toward the alcove where Laura was. Without being too obvious about it, Elly and I strolled along behind them. When we approached the alcove, I saw that Linda was having a whispered but urgent conversation with her sister. Judging by her defiant expression, Laura wasn't having any part of whatever Linda was saying to her.

The two couples came into the alcove.

Linda nodded at her sister, glanced at the two couples, paused just a moment, then strode to where Elly and I stood in the hallway, watching.

The couples approached Laura.

Laura beamed happily.

Chapter Twenty

I talked very little as we drove back to Elly's house after the art show. Elly honored my silence, realizing that I was mulling over what to do next. I did mumble that I needed to call Balls. Elly nodded. When we got to her house and went inside, her mother was in the living room watching television. It was some program with singing, maybe *American Idol* or one of those shows. Mrs. Pedersen smiled and asked how was the art show.

"Very nice," Elly said, "and the good news is that Laura Shackleford sold two of her paintings. She was excited." Then she nodded toward the back. "Martin do all right?"

"Went right to sleep. And I'm about ready to go on back myself if you all wanted to sit in here a spell."

"Oh, no," I said, "I need to get on back. I've got to, to do some work."

"And make a call," Elly said, watching my face.

I nodded.

The Pedersens' phone rang. Mother and daughter both exchanged puzzled looks. I glanced at my watch. It was shortly before nine. Mrs. Pedersen answered the phone and then handed it to Elly, with a slight look of anxiety. "It's Linda," she said.

Elly took the phone. I stood there waiting. Elly kept her eyes on me while she talked. "I see. Lone Cedar. With all four of them. The two couples." She listened a moment or two, little wrinkles across her brow. "But she's got her own car." Another pause. "She promised? Promised to come straight home afterwards? Good. If she means it . . . Just a minute. Hold on." To me, she said, "Laura got invited to dinner by those two couples." Elly bit her lower lip. "Linda wants to know if you think you ought to, you know, show up at the restaurant."

"Jeeze, I don't . . . okay, tell her I'll go wait in the parking lot. I know Laura's car. I'll wait, out of sight, make sure she gets in it and goes home."

Elly relayed that information to Linda. She said, "I know, Linda, and I'll tell him how much you appreciate it. He'll call you, or I will. Don't worry."

Sensing our concern, Mrs. Pedersen looked from one of us to the other. But Elly didn't take the time to explain to her. To me, she said, "Going to call Agent Twiddy?"

"Right now," I said. I flipped open my cell and punched in his number. The signal was weak. Elly pointed to the front porch and I stepped outside just as he answered.

The gruff, "Yeah?"

I told him about the visit to the Art Council's show, and the presence of the two couples and how they came on to Laura Shackleford. Balls knows Linda, but not her sister. I told him Laura had joined the couples at Lone Cedar restaurant and that I was going to stakeout her car in the parking lot, make sure she went home and not somewhere else with the couples.

"Good," Balls said. "I'm still in Elizabeth City. Be here probably tomorrow. But, Weav, don't do anything stupid if she goes off with them. Just call me and I'll get someone from Dare County to pick her up."

"Pick her up? How?"

"I'll drum up something. You just don't try to play Mr. Hero."

"Uh-huh."

"I mean it, damnit! I still think one of them has a hand-gun, and they obviously know how to use it."

"Okay, okay. I'll hang back." We clicked off. I hoped, of course, that Laura would finish her meal or drinks or whatever they were having, get in her car, and head home. I went back inside. Elly stood and talked to her mother, who remained seated in the upholstered chair near the muted television. The picture alternated between a panel of judges and the audience applauding, all without sound.

"You talked with him?"

I nodded. "He's still in Elizabeth City. I told him what I was going to do."

"And?"

I chuckled. "He told me not to try to play Mr. Hero."

She stared at me with a sort of schoolmarm scowl. "Harrison . . ."

"I promised him I wouldn't."

"Promise me."

"Promise," I said. "Besides, probably no need to be worried. She'll have dinner or dessert or something and head home."

Mrs. Pedersen followed our conversation. Worry showed on her face.

"I'd better head on over," I said.

"Want me to go with you?"

"No! Absolutely not." Then, more softly, I said, "No need, really."

"Stay in touch with me by phone. I won't go to sleep until this is over."

I said I would and I gave Elly a light kiss goodnight. It would have been more of a kiss, but not with mama present.

I drove through Manteo and swung left onto US 64-264 toward the beaches. Crossing over the Washington Baum Bridge I could see lights of Nags Head ahead of me and to the left. I always glanced over my right shoulder to see the fewer lights all the way down at Wanchese. I crossed "Little Bridge" and a short distance on my right was the Lone Cedar. As late as it was, the parking lot had thinned out considerably. I made one pass through the lot and spotted

Laura's older Toyota. A few spaces away was a Mercedes SUV with Florida tags. I knew it belonged to one of the couples. I turned around and backed into a space far enough away from both of the vehicles not to be noticed, but close enough to see clearly when they emerged from the restaurant. I sat there waiting. I wished I'd gone to the bathroom at Elly's before I got started on this business.

Judging by what Linda had said to Elly, her sister had been here about an hour or so. Surely they would be closing before long. I slumped down in my seat, but kept an eye constantly on the front door. A couple came out and went to their car. Then shortly four young people came out. I could hear one of the women laughing as she hung on to her escort's arm.

Less than five minutes later, while I squirmed uncomfortably and tried not to think about needing to pee, five people came out—the two couples and Laura. With my window down I could hear their animated talking but I couldn't make out what they were saying. They stopped close to the Mercedes and continued their conversation. Laura said something and pointed to her nearby car. She shook hands with Stan and Karl and then Velda gave her a quick hug.

Good. It certainly appeared they were saying their goodbyes. Karl leaned in closer and said something else to Laura and then gave her something of an awkward and quick hug. Laura waved her hand and started toward her car. She stopped when one of them—Stan or Karl—called something to her and she nodded and waved again.

The two couples began loading into the Mercedes and Laura got in her Toyota. I waited until their engines started and I turned my ignition on but kept my headlights off for the moment. The Mercedes backed out and then pulled toward the beach side of the parking lot; Laura came toward me, headed back toward Manteo. Good, again. I eased out so I was in position to follow Laura. She made her left turn toward Manteo and her home. The Mercedes was almost out of sight headed in the opposite direction. I watched until Laura got close to Little Bridge, heading across the causeway and then Roanoke Sound.

I was so relieved I'd momentarily forgotten the increasing need to answer a call of nature. But then the urgency returned and I headed for home, in the same direction the two couples had headed. I flipped open my phone and speed-dialed Elly. She answered almost immediately.

"I'm certainly relieved," she said.

"Well, I'm heading home as fast as I can so I can relieve myself."

She didn't catch it at first, and then she laughed and said, "Oh. One of the hazards of a stakeout, huh?"

"Yes."

She said, "I'll call Linda right now and tell her Laura is on her way home."

Then, "Oh, Linda called again a little while ago. She was concerned because she maybe hadn't said enough about the two couples to Laura. She said she didn't mention anything about, you know, your suspicions."

"As it turns out, that's probably just as well." I added, "I don't think Balls would want us spreading that word."

I thought about calling Balls. But I put the cell down long enough to get around a couple of cars, one in the right lane and then cut back to pass on the right one that was in the inside lane. I drove faster than I normally did, but I needed to get home. I had a clear road ahead of me past Jockey's Ridge. Then my cell rang, playing the whistled theme from the *Andy Griffith Show*. After all, I was here in the area where Andy Griffith had made his home.

It was Balls. "I was thinking of calling you. Thought I'd wait until morning." I gave him a rundown of my amateur stakeout, the fact that Laura was heading home, and that she was not told details of our suspicions about the two couples.

"Good," he said. "I hope to be back over there tomorrow or tomorrow night. Finally winding up this business here in Elizabeth City." As if musing to himself, he muttered, "Want to get back on this hogtieing, and Stafford slaying. Can't keep letting it get colder and colder." Another pause. "Don't want those couples to slip away, head out on another one of their caravans." I thought he was about to sign off, and then he said, "The fact that this sister of Linda's didn't take off with the couples tonight, doesn't necessarily mean they're through with her. Their pattern has been to butter some gal up and then . . ."

"Right," I said. "But how much do you want me, or Linda, to say to her sister?"

"Nothing yet. But keep an eye on it—until I get there."

I didn't know how in the hell I was to "keep an eye on it." So I said, a touch of irritation in my voice, "You want me to go to Laura and tell her to stay damn well away from these folks?"

"Just cool it, Weav. Let me handle it. But have Linda let you know what her sister is up to, if anything. Maybe nothing, if we're lucky."

"And if the sister is lucky," I said, and we signed off. I made it home in record time and didn't waste a minute rushing up the stairs and to the bathroom. I heard Janey chirping and I called out, "Talk to you in a minute, Jancy."

I came back into the living room and spoke to Janey. I gave her some fresh water. I never could figure out how she could get in position to poop in her water dish that was like a cone affixed to the side of her cage. She bobbed her head and made sounds almost like talking. "Okay," I said, "I'll give you a sprig of millet seeds."

I locked up and then checked e-mail to see if Rose, my editor, had sent anything urgent. Nothing there unless I was interested in meeting singles named Heather and Amber in the Norfolk area, or some such place. Well, the "some such place" went straight to spam. Sorry about that, Heather and Amber. I went to bed and slept a lot more soundly than I expected to.

The next morning promised to be another lovely late spring day, sunny, very light breeze out of the northwest, and not too hot nor humid. I went out on the front deck with a fresh cup of coffee.

And then I got a call from my nemesis, prosecutor Rick Schweikert.

"Mr. Weaver," he said, "I've been looking into the senseless slaying of young Jarvis Stafford."

Uh-oh, I thought. Why was he calling me about this? All crimes for Schweikert were senseless, or heinous, or some such adjective.

"I was wondering, Mr. Weaver, if you could come into town at your convenience so we can talk about this?"

Hmm. Now that was unusually polite for Schweikert, especially in regards to how he usually dealt with me. He didn't like me anymore than I liked him. "What's up, Rick? Agent Twiddy is handling the investigation on that."

"Oh, I know," he said. "But you did have some contact with the late Jarvis Stafford. I've checked into his back-ground, and I see that he had been charged earlier over near Goldsboro with extortion, and I thought you might know something about whether a similar activity—or attempted activity—might have contributed to his fate."

I was silent for a moment. "What's that got to do with me?"

"I know you are close to Agent Twiddy and that the two of you have been looking into the tragic killing of that young woman—the woman you just *happened* to find—over at Buffalo City."

He wasn't letting that go. I said, "Well why not talk with Agent Twiddy about it?"

"I've tried to get him but he's involved in a matter over in Elizabeth City, and I thought you and I might . . ."

"Rick, all due respect, but I'm just a bystander in all of this and I really don't have anything else to contribute to it. Besides, I know that Agent Twiddy would be upset with me, to put it mildly, if I started nosing into it with you."

"I see." He was silent again and I wasn't sure but what he was ready to hang up. Then he said, "Okay, Mr. Weaver.

You don't need to come in. Not now." He made a little clucking sound. "But remember this, Mr. Weaver, I am very much concerned that you seem always to be involved with people who manage to get themselves killed. And you find too many bodies to make me comfortable."

I gripped the handset of the phone so tightly my knuckles turned white. I managed to control my voice. "Rick, I've got things to do and I'm going to pretend that this conversation—as similar as it is to others I've had with you—never, ever occurred. Goodbye."

I stood there by the phone, staring at it, daring it to ring again. It didn't.

I heard Janey chirping away in her cage. As clear as day she said one of the two words she can mimic perfectly: "Bitch."

I puffed out a laugh. "My sentiments exactly, Janey."

Chapter Twenty-One

Later that morning I called Elly at the Register of Deeds office. "You able to go to lunch with me?"

"I'd love to," she said, "but Linda called and asked me first. Want to go with us?"

"That'd be good," I said. "I'd like to talk with her more about last night and my concerns about her sister and those couples."

"And I know she'd like to talk with you too."

We agreed to meet at noon at Ortega'z in downtown Manteo.

I got there a few minutes early and secured a table for us. Shortly after twelve Elly and Linda came into the restaurant together. They were engaged in conversation as they entered, stopped just inside the doorway and then saw me, and headed for my table. I stood and gave Elly a quick hug and shook hands with Linda. Elly wore a white cotton blouse and trim tan slacks, sandals. I was always pleased with how fresh she looked.

Linda, by contrast, was in a baggy, short-sleeve pullover shirt and jeans. She carried her reporter's notebook and camera. "Don't I get a hug, too?" Linda said, that big grin on her face.

So I gave her an exaggerated bear hug.

"More like it," she said.

A young man, who identified himself as Brian, brought

us menus and said he would be our server. All three of us ordered sweet tea and settled almost simultaneously on the chicken quesadias. "Well, that's certainly not too complicated," Brian said, smiled, and left to place our order with the kitchen.

On his return trip he brought our iced tea.

Elly was seated beside me. Linda, sitting opposite us, leaned forward, her elbows on the table. She spoke directly to me. "Scoop, I certainly appreciate your keeping an eye on Laura last night. God knows somebody needs to keep check on her . . . at all times."

I nodded. "I understand you didn't say anything to Laura about why we were concerned about her being with the couples."

"No, I didn't. Maybe it would have done more good if I had." She leaned back, and shook her head. "Nope, it wouldn't have," she said. "Fact is, it would probably have made it worse. She'd think that was exciting. All the more reason to schmooze with them." She shook her head again.

Elly displayed the trace of a knowing smile, and nodded her head. She turned to me. "Everything going okay? Anything happening today?"

"Not really," I said. "Had a courtesy call from Rick Schweikert, suggesting maybe we chat a bit. But I—almost politely—declined."

Elly raised one eyebrow, but made no comment.

"Your buddy, huh?" Linda said.

Brian brought our food. He put down three small containers of sour cream. "Need anymore salsa, let me know." He stood there a couple of beats and surveyed our table, making sure all was in order. "Enjoy," he said, and hurried away.

Elly said, "Linda says Laura is home today painting away. Called in sick at work so she could concentrate on her artwork."

"Yeah," Linda said, bending over her food and giving it full attention, "she sells two paintings and now she's going to be a famous artist."

"But, Linda," Elly said, "you know it was exciting for her, and really is a compliment to her."

"I know, I know," Linda said. "I didn't mean to sound mean." She looked up at us and I thought there was the trace of a tear in her eye. "I just want the best for her. You know I love her. She's my little sister, but she does drive me nuts sometimes. She's so . . . so flighty, or boy crazy. Man crazy, I guess it is. She's twenty-two now . . ." Almost under her breath, she added, ". . . going on thirteen."

Before we finished eating, Linda said, "Weav, let me give you my cell number, just in case there's something else you want me to tell Laura. You know, more details that'll put some sense into her head."

I entered her number in my cell phone memory.

"That was good," Linda said, and started into her small wallet she had in the back pocket of her jeans.

"No, no," I said. "This is on me."

Both of them thanked me. Then Linda said, "I've got to run to a meeting of the planning committee. Exciting stuff. Right?" She pushed back from the table. "Thanks again for lunch."

"I'll have to go in a minute, too," Elly said. But she didn't make any movement toward getting up.

When Linda left, Elly turned to me and said, "And what are your plans this afternoon? Keeping us safe from murder and mayhem?"

"And preserving Truth, Justice, and the American Way," I said.

She chuckled, gazed into my eyes. "We're a couple now, aren't we?"

I touched her arm. "I think we've been a couple for some time. Even before . . ."

"I do, too," she said. She grinned. "And I'll tell you one thing—Scoop—you are really something." She actually blushed then. "I'd better get back to work, quit thinking about that."

On the way back to my house in Kill Devil Hills, I took the Beach Road, which was quieter, sparse traffic, giving me time to think, mull over where we stood with the investigation—and where Elly and I stood. I felt good about Elly and me. I could see down the road for us and how it could get better and better, how we would get closer all the time. I even let myself think about the possibility of marriage, of living together from now on. That made me smile with a good feeling.

But then my mind shifted to thinking about the murders, the fact that somehow these two couples—or one of them— were involved. And a resolution didn't seem any closer than it was in the beginning. My smile faded.

When I got up to the Kill Devil Hills bathhouse, I pulled into the parking lot and cut the engine. Only a few other cars were parked there. I walked out on the wooden ramp and deck overlooking the ocean, my church pew for meditation. The tide had turned. Waves rolled in with a soft roar, churning up the beach sand, and receding. The surf was greenish up close to shore but reflecting the blue sky out a hundred yards or more. The light wind from the west flattened the ocean as much as it ever gets flattened here at the Outer Banks. I breathed in deeply, and I stood there for several minutes. But my usual calm at the edge of the ocean didn't come to me.

I couldn't shake the frustration over the stalemate in solving the killings—the one up at Mattaskeet, the one here, and the shooting of Jarvis Stafford. Plus there was murder, also, and similar in Florida, where two of the couples were from. I shook my head and went back to the parking area. My church hadn't worked for me this time.

At my house, I walked slowly up the outside stairs. Maybe if I practiced the bass a bit, played some scales. I spoke to Janey. Even she appeared subdued. I tightened and rosined my bow, picked up my bass and leaned it into me. I tuned it using harmonics, and started desultorily playing major scales.

By six that evening I finally began to think about what I would fix for supper. I wasn't at all hungry, but I knew I needed to eat. I figured maybe soup and a salad; I'd had protein at lunch. Oh, well, I'd think about it later. Janey muttered her muted chirping sounds, sitting on one of her perches all fluffed up. "You're sort of down, too," I said. She ignored me.

Then, just as I've had it happen before when things seem the bleakest and at a complete standstill, things begin to happen. Pieces began to fall in place.

First there was a call from Linda. Her voice came fast, words tumbling on top of one another. "Hey, Weav, that crazy sister is at it again and maybe we need to do something, see if we can get some sense in her head if that's possible."

"Hold on a minute, Linda. Slow down. Start all over again."

"Sorry." She took an audible breath. "I started not to call you at all. Didn't want to bug you. But Laura has gone to meet those couples. Well, meet one of them. They called her and want her third painting."

"Which couple?"

"The ones who bought the other two pictures. Karl and Velda something."

"Well, that in itself is not too bad." But then something clicked. "You said 'meet them.' Meet them where?"

"That's just it. They asked her to come up to Duck, bring the painting, then they'll take her to dinner."

I think I muttered, "Oh, shit."

Janey livened up and said, "Shit."

I said, "What about the other couple?"

"She didn't mention them. I think it's just Karl and Velda."

"That's not good, Linda," I said, as if she didn't suspect it also. "Did she say where she was to meet them? Where she'll meet them with the painting?"

Linda sounded as if she might be fighting back a sob.

"At their place. I told her something about what you suspect—in fact I broke your confidence and I told her a *lot* of what you suspect—and she just blew me off, saying I'd make up anything to keep her from expanding herself. That's what she said, expanding herself."

"You got an address?"

"Yes, I did manage to get her to tell me where she would be. I wrote it down."

"Give it to me," I said.

She read me the address. It was just as I expected, the one Balls and had pointed out to me that night.

She said, "What are you going to do?"

"I honestly don't know, Linda. But I'm going up there. I'll think of something. Make up a story, maybe an emergency at home. Something."

"Can I go with you?"

"No need to, Linda. In fact, may be best if you don't. Maybe she'll listen to me—instead of her big sister."

"I could get up to your place in twenty minutes or so."

"How long has she been gone?"

"That's the thing. She's been there now an hour or more. I know maybe I should have called you right away, but . . ." Her voice trailed off, and I saw no sense in making her feel more apprehensive than she already did.

More to myself than to Linda, I said, "I'll need to call Balls . . . Agent Twiddy to tell him where I'm going, and why."

Then I heard a call-waiting click on my phone line. "Hold on just a second, Linda. That could be Agent Twiddy right now. He was supposed to call." I clicked over. It was Balls.

As soon as I spoke, an excited Balls said, "My man, I've got news for you—these killings have gone international."

And so the second happening had tumbled forth.

"Hold on, Balls," I said. "I've got what may be a *local* emergency on the other line."

"What?"

"Be right back with you. Need to talk to you about local stuff right away. International may have to wait." I clicked over to Linda. "Linda, stay right near the phone. That's Agent Twiddy on the other line. I'll call you back."

"Okay, okay," she said.

I switched to Balls and spoke hurriedly. "One of the couples, Karl and Velda Simpkins, have got Linda Shackleford's young sister at their place tonight in Duck. Supposed to be buying her artwork, treating her to dinner—and I don't like it at all."

"When did she go there?"

"An hour or so ago." I took a breath. "Where are you?"

"Just getting ready to leave Elizabeth City."

"What's this about international?"

"Let's deal with local first," he said, echoing my sentiments.

"I think I need to go to Duck."

"Yeah, and what you going to do when you get there?"

I held the phone tightly against my ear, but shook my head. "I don't know," I said. It sounded lame.

"That's just it. It'll take me close to an hour to get there but I can legitimately interview them." Then he added the obvious: "You can't."

"But an hour . . ." I said.

"Take you twenty minutes to get there."

"Twelve or fifteen," I said.

"Yeah, and what you gonna say to them? 'I've come to take Linda's little sister home'?"

He had a point, and I knew it. Just the same, doing nothing certainly didn't suit me. I remembered I had to call Linda back. But then, "What about the international?"

"Remember that conference in Washington I went to last winter? Law enforcement from all over the world. Big deal. I met this detective from France. Paris. He and I hit it off real good." He took a breath. "Well, he called me this evening. Middle of the night over there. He'd read in one of the dispatches about our hogtieing cases." Then he dropped the bomb: "He had a similar one over there." Then the bomb went off: "This past April a year ago."

"Oh, crap," I said. "Karl and Velda were in Paris last April."

I heard his intake of breath. "Oh, boy, oh boy," he said quietly.

"Yeah. That's what I think."

"While the victim over there wasn't exactly hogtied, she was nude, had ropes around her, thrown late at night along the walkways of the Seine, the river over there in Paris . . . France."

"I'm going up to Duck. Can't wait."

"Hold on . . . I'm on my way."

But I didn't hold on. I grabbed my car keys and rushed out the door, throwing the night latch on. Didn't bother to cut out any of the lights. I jumped in my Subaru and punched in Linda's number as I backed out of the carport and swung around in the cul-de-sac. She answered before I'd reached the Bypass. "I'm on my way up there, Linda," I said. She started to say something but I said, "Can't talk. Got to drive." I clicked off and drove well above the speed limit, headed to Duck.

What I was going to do when I got to Karl and Velda's rental, I had no clue, except that I was on a hell-bent-for-leather mission to get Laura out of there.

When I got close to Mile Post 1, I swung to the right onto Duck Road. Balls would have to come all the way to this intersection before he could make what amounted to a U-turn and head back up toward Duck. To myself I muttered, "If they'd ever get that damn mid-county bridge built Balls would be able to cut across in Currituck County and get there a lot quicker."

The speed limit on Duck Road is forty-five. I was going close to sixty. Then approaching the Duck city limits, the posted speed limit drops to thirty-five, then twenty-five. I ignored the signs and hoped one of the town cops wouldn't interfere. The road curves a bit in Duck. My tires fairly sang as I made the curves, passing Duck Deli, Scarborough Faire, and other businesses. Then I saw the road with a cutesy nautical name that led into the huge houses.

I pulled into a reserved "No Parking" space and clicked the lock button on my key fob as I strode toward the beige and light blue house that rose like a castle above the sand dunes, giving the upper floors a dramatic view of the ocean.

I bounded up a set of stairs to the second level. There was a 2-A on the doorway. No other entrance doors were on this level or approachable by the stairway I took. Hoping this was the apartment unit, I paused just a moment, catching my breath.

Then I pounded on the door.

I heard nothing. I pounded again.

I eyed the door and wondered if I could shoulder it open, bust it down.

But the door opened.

There stood Karl Simpkins, that sleepy cast to his round eyes. He wore what looked like silk navy blue lounging pajama bottoms and a white pullover shirt of the same material. "We kind of thought you just might show up. Come on in." He smiled and, gently pushing the door shut, he stepped back from the doorway.

Chapter Twenty-Two

Being ushered in so politely was the last thing I had expected. The living room was spacious and tastefully furnished in expensive beach-themed furniture: pastel colors, overstuffed pillows, rattan and wicker chairs and sofa. Large picture windows, one of them open, overlooked ocean. From lights outside I could see the surf roiling up on the beach.

Karl stood there smiling at me. "Catch your breath," he said.

"Listen, I've come to get Laura Shackleford. Her sister . . . there's an emergency . . . at home . . ." I was making it up as I stammered. I could feel the perspiration running down my sides.

Then Velda glided into the living room from a doorway off to the right. She stood there a moment, then continued on into the living room, leaving the door she had exited partially open. She moved lazily, her head tilted to one side, a sensual smile playing on her lips. Not a care in the world. She held her hands clasped casually behind her, accentuating the sheerness of the short silk negligee. Her breasts and the rest of her body were visible through the material.

Velda turned her face toward Karl, the smile still there. "You might as well tell him that won't be possible, Karl."

I stared at her. "What? What won't be possible?"

Velda shrugged. "Taking Laura." There was almost a soft little chuckle. "She's . . . she's resting. Taking a little nap." She inclined her head toward the door she had just come through.

I stepped forward, my fists clinched. I could see into the other room. I drew in my breath. I felt my heart pounding. "What the . . ." My eyes were wide. I stared into the room. There, stretched out spread-eagle and motionless on a queen-size bed, with ropes affixed to her wrists and her ankles, lay a nude Laura Shackleford.

I spun around to face Karl and then Velda. I glared at them. Then I took two long strides toward the other room. But Velda stepped in front of me. I started to shove her out of the way.

But she got my attention.

One of her hands came out from behind her back and she pointed a pistol dead center at my chest.

"She's just resting a bit," Velda said. "I think she drank too much." That insolent smile gave an evil cast to her face. "So stand right there and don't bother her."

The pistol she pointed at me appeared to be a .22 with a suppressor screwed onto the muzzle, giving it extra length, and considerably less noise when fired.

Karl came over from behind me to stand next to his wife. Both of them looked at me like we were having a pleasant conversation.

My chest heaved with every breath. I wiped perspiration off of my forehead with my arm, then stood there with my arms by my side, but my body tensed. I contemplated a tackling leap onto Velda.

Karl read my thoughts. "Mr. Weaver, I really should warn you. Velda is an excellent shot, and very, very quick. My advice: Don't try something stupid."

Velda said, "We'd like for you to take a seat in that chair behind you."

I glanced over my shoulder but then quickly back at the two of them. The chair behind me had a puffy seat cushion and wicker arms.

"Go ahead," she said. "You'll be more comfy." She

made a nudging motion with the pistol, as if prodding me to sit.

I stepped back until I felt the edge of the chair against my legs. I eased myself down.

"Now that's better," Karl said.

My voice was now under more control. "You two don't really think you can get away with this, do you?"

She gave that little tilt to her head. "Oh, it doesn't really make much difference to us now. We've had a good run at it." She spoke to Karl. "Haven't we, darling?"

He licked his lips. "Yes, we have." He almost squirmed. "Yes, we have," he repeated.

"And we've got plans, Mr. Weaver. It may not end here at all. It just might end at your house."

"What the hell you talking about?"

"We may all pay a visit to your house. We've known for some time where you live. And little Laura, our budding artist, is going to be asleep for a while longer." Velda actually chuckled. "Who knows? She may not wake up." Velda took a step closer to me, that pistol still leveled at my chest. I thought about the three slugs in Jarvis Stafford's chest, and I took an involuntary gulp of air.

Without taking her eyes off of me, she spoke to Karl. "Would you get a section of that rope, dear?"

He nodded and stepped out of my line of vision, and then reappeared with a coil of rope like that they had used on Laura. He twisted it in his hands, almost stroking it.

"Just suppose, Mr. Weaver," Velda said, "that our nude little Laura is found in *your* bed and that you—the sex-crazed pervert that you are—are found there beside her—strangled, the victim of your own failed attempt at auto-eroticism."

Karl snickered, playing more eagerly with the rope.

I found my voice again. Maybe aggression on my part would help. "No sense in telling you that you're both sick. You know that. But what about your partners, Stan and his wife? They in on it with you?"

"Oh, heavens no," Velda said.

"They're too uptight to get the fun out of this that we do," Karl said.

"And we think they'll be leaving the caravan also," Velda said. "A shame. We could have had them enjoy some of this with us, which is what we thought would happen in the beginning."

She came closer, over to the side of my chair, and pressed the pistol against my temple. I realized I was biting my lower lip and I tried to stop. I could smell her cologne and I was fully aware that she was naked under the sheer negligee. "The rope, Karl, please."

He scurried over to the other side of my chair. Velda pulled the pistol back an inch or so as he dropped a loop of rope over my head and around my neck. He had tied a slipknot, and he tightened the noose. It didn't bite into my neck but I could feel the pressure of the rope against my sweat soaked skin. He held the other end of the rope wrapped around his wrist.

I wanted to keep them talking, delaying the inevitable as long as possible. I knew that Balls had to be racing to get here. If we weren't here, he wouldn't know where in the hell to look. The last place he would search would be my own house. We had to stay here as long as possible. Maybe if I could get them to keep talking, bragging about their little games, as they call these horrors that they've committed.

"So, not only the killing here and up at Mattaskeet, but at least two in Florida—and Paris."

Velda actually brightened. "Oh, you know about Paris. My, my, that's something. How did you find out about that? It doesn't really matter, of course. And, well, it didn't go off exactly as we'd planned . . ."

I interrupted: "No, the poor woman wasn't hogtied."

"We had to rush it a bit at the end. But we had a lovely time in Paris. I love Paris."

Stalling for more time, I said, "What about here at the Outer Banks? Why did you come here?" My mouth was so dry I could hardly get the words out.

Karl chuckled. "Shall I tell him, dear?"

"Go ahead."

"We saw you there in Mattaskeet," Karl said, "and got fascinated with the fact that you were looking into the murder there—but then you gave up," Karl said. "My sweet wife thought it would increase our little game if we followed you here and did the same sort of thing. You know, had a party with a willing young woman. The whole thing would probably end up in one of your books."

Velda smiled. "We knew you were going to go kayaking at Buffalo City that morning."

I shook my head and tried to spit out the words: "You two are crazy . . . sick . . ."

Velda made a grunting sound, followed quickly with a hard slap across my face with the barrel of the pistol. It stung and I felt a trickle of blood ooze down from my cheekbone. "Don't be insulting," she hissed.

Karl appeared to squirm with pleasure.

I thought now or never. I tensed my legs to spring from the chair, but Velda jammed the muzzle of the pistol into my right ear. The edge of the suppressor snagged part of my ear and I winced. "Stay still. Real still," she said.

"Dear, we'd better get ready to go," Karl said, as casually as if it was a dinner date they had planned.

"Yes, we'll have to carry our naked Miss Shackleford," Velda said. "Go ahead and untie her. She's not going to wake up for some time—" There was that lazy little laugh of hers. "—if ever."

She eased back on the muzzle of the pistol. "Mr. Weaver here is going to help us."

"What the hell makes you think I'm going to help?"

The pistol cracked me across the bridge of my nose, and she poked me again in the face with it. "This is what's going to make you help us."

My only chance to overpower Velda and her pistol could occur, I knew, during the struggle to get Laura out of the bed and down the stairs. Perhaps, just perhaps, there might be enough activity to distract Karl and Velda so I could make a move. At the same time, I didn't want to jeopardize Laura any more than possible. Too, I hoped that any minute Balls might arrive from Elizabeth City. I wasn't at all sure what he could do if he walked into this situation, but there was certainly no hope apparent from the way things stood now.

"Get up from there," Velda commanded, indicating with a wave of the muzzle from me toward the bedroom where Laura lay nude and as still as death. It was clear that was the path I was to take.

I rose from the chair slowly, keeping my eyes on Velda. The noose was loosely around my neck, the end of the rope on the floor where Karl had dropped it. Velda picked up the end. Karl stood off to one side, keeping a close watch. I used my right forearm to wipe a mixture of sweat and blood from my cheek.

Velda stayed behind me as I moved toward the bedroom. Velda had the pistol pointed at the center of my back and I could feel that she had a good grip on the rope. Between the pistol and the rope, any sudden move on my part and that would be it.

Karl moved ahead of us and entered the bedroom and began untying the ropes from Laura's ankles and wrists. She still didn't move, except to turn her head slightly to one side, as if she had been disturbed from a deep sleep. At least she was alive . . . for now.

"Hold it right there," Velda said. "Wait for Karl to get her ready for you to pick up." Then she nudged me with the pistol, gently, as if to get my attention. "Isn't she lovely, though? Huh? You like looking at her?" There was that low chuckle again. "You can understand why we've had so much fun."

"I can understand how sick you are," I muttered.

"I'm not going to hit you again, even though you *are* insulting," she said. "We don't want you to look too beat up once you're discovered after your botched effort at auto-eroticism. And a dead nude female by your side."

Karl had finished untying Laura and stood beside the bed, a sleepy smile on his face. He kept looking at Laura, his gaze sweeping over her, up and down.

"Okay," Velda said, "pull her over to you and get her on her feet. You won't have to carry her probably. You can support her and move her along like she's sleepwalking.

I pulled Laura to the edge of the bed by one arm. She made a faint moaning sound as if someone disturbed. Bending over, I looped her left arm over my shoulder and lifted her toward me and off the bed. Her feet came to the floor and while her legs didn't support her fully, she was not deadweight. At least not yet.

With her body pressed against me, I could feel how sweat-soaked my shirt was.

"They look cute, don't they, Karl? Like a loving couple."

Karl snickered. He held a coil of rope in his hands and twisted it back and forth.

"Let's get started," Velda said. "Toward the door." She added, either to herself or to Karl, "It's plenty dark. We'll keep the outside light turned off." With the pistol and a slight tug on the rope, she motioned me forward.

Half dragging her, half walking her, I moved forward with a naked Laura up against me. Karl was two or three paces ahead of us.

He flipped a light switch off and opened the door to the stairway landing. He uttered a gasp, and stepped back quickly.

Standing right there, his hand raised to knock on the door, was Stan. His wife beside him. She clutched his arm. "Oh, my God," she said.

"What . . . what the hell's going on?" Stan stammered.

"Oh . . ." his wife moaned. She looked like she might collapse, that brittle face coming all undone. "I told you, Stan. Just like Denise said. They *are* involved in all this . . ."

Karl kept looking back and forth to the couple in front of

him and to Velda, as if he needed instruction. Velda kept her cool. She motioned with the pistol. "Don't just stand there. Come on in. Join the party."

Stan's wife's eyes looked like they might pop out of her head. "Party? Party? What in God's name are you doing, Velda?"

Then I heard the pounding of footsteps coming up the stairway. Someone sprinting up the steps. A big someone. Then, there framed in the doorway, was Balls, his big .45 caliber Glock out and at the ready.

"My, my," Velda said. "This looks like what they'd call a Mexican standoff."

Chapter Twenty-Three

Balls swept his gaze quickly around the room and at all of us standing there. At the same time, he kept the Glock trained mostly on Velda.

"Stan and his wife aren't involved," I managed to blurt out.

Velda gave the rope a jerk. "Shut up," she hissed.

Stan and Becky moved two or three steps to the side, just inside the living room.

Balls concentrated on Velda and Karl.

Then Velda jammed the muzzle of her pistol against my left temple. Her voice was level, controlled: "I think it would be a good idea, detective, to lower that wicked looking pistol of yours."

Balls glared at her. He kept his weapon aimed dead center at Velda. "It's all over for you two now," he said. "There's no way you can get out of this."

"You don't want your buddy here to take a bullet in the head, do you?"

Laura made another of her moaning sounds as if she might be trying to wake up. Her arm was over my left shoulder; I held her waist with my right hand, supporting her.

I knew that if I was to make a move, now was the time. It had to be now.

I let go of Laura's waist and she began to slump forward. I twisted my body so she began to collapse partly in front of me. Her upper body swung to the left. Her head and torso banged against Velda's legs.

This distracted Velda enough so momentarily she moved the muzzle of the pistol away from my temple to glance down quickly at Laura, crumpling at her feet.

In that instant I lunged and grabbed Velda's right wrist, forcing the pistol to aim toward the ceiling.

There was the suppressed pow-sound of her weapon discharging into the air.

Then there was a much louder gunshot. From Balls's weapon. And Velda made a grunting sound and she went over backward.

Karl screamed, "Velda . . . Velda . . ." And he dropped the ropes and scurried to his wife. One of her legs was bent under her, the other outstretched. Her negligee was hiked up. Blood pumped from her chest, beginning to cover the upper part of her gown. Karl acted like he didn't know what to do. He touched her face and then he pulled the hem of her negligee down, covering her slightly. "Oh, Velda," he said. He looked up at Balls, a pleading expression on his face.

Balls kept the Glock trained on the two of them. The pistol was still in her outstretched hand. "Kick that pistol away," Balls said, his voice almost a monotone.

My ears still rang from the explosion of Balls' weapon.

Karl didn't move. So I reached over with my foot and pushed the pistol from Velda's hand. Karl hovered over Velda. The blood had stopped pumping, but still spreading, and she was very still.

Becky sank into a chair near the door. Stan stood beside her, a dazed, almost vacant expression on his face.

Balls, his lips drawn tightly, the gun still at the ready, moved forward and with one foot pushed Velda's pistol farther away. He reached down and felt for a pulse on Velda's neck. He moved his hand back, nudged Karl with the muzzle of his gun, and said softly, "Stand up and put your hands behind your back." From underneath his windbreaker, Balls brought out a pair of handcuffs and with a swift motion secured Karl's wrists.

Tears rolled down Karl's cheeks and he kept looking at Velda's lifeless body.

To me, Balls said, "Get Linda's sister up, on to the sofa . . . cover her up with something."

I started trying to pick her up. My hands trembled and my arms felt weak. Balls inclined his head toward Stan. "Help him," Balls said. Stan hurried over and between us we picked up Laura and stretched her out on the sofa. Becky appeared at our side with an afghan she pulled off one of the chairs. She covered Laura.

Laura's eyes flickered open for a moment. She looked around, puzzled, then drifted off again.

Balls had his cell phone out, making the necessary calls.

When he clicked off his phone and put it back on his belt, he turned to me. "That was a gutsy—and stupid—move that you made."

I nodded.

He looked down at Velda. He shook his head.

I could imagine some of the emotions running through him.

Plenty of emotions ran through me. Suddenly my legs felt wobbly and I sat on one of the chairs nearest me. "A hell of a night," I mumbled.

"Yeah," Balls said. There was very little life in his voice. "A hell of a night." He took a deep breath as if to clear his feelings, regain control. "But it's over. It's all over."

I nodded and stared at the floor.

A very short time later I heard the beginning sound of sirens, their high-pitched wail getting closer, like a scream of lament in the night.

The End

Epilogue

Balls had to go through the official administrative hearing about the shooting of Velda Simpkins. But with all of the witnesses there, and a disposition of Karl Simpkins, it went smoothly and Balls was cleared of any wrongdoing, of course. In his mind, though, it weighed heavily, I could tell. In all of his years of service, he had to shoot only one other human being, and that person was wounded only in the leg.

The sick episodes of Karl and Velda were ended. His trial is coming up shortly. He is putting much of the blame on Velda, saying he just went along with her. He'll get maybe life, but not the death penalty, in all probability. Stan and Becky were cleared of any involvement, as were Denise and Dewey Farrish.

Karl admitted that Jarvis Stafford had called them after that dinner. They had met him out on the beach. Karl claimed Jarvis was trying to get them to give him money—five thousand dollars—not to go to the police with the fact that they had invited Sharon Dawson up to their apartment. He said Velda appeared to be reaching in her purse but she pulled out the .22 caliber pistol with the suppressor on it and fired three times point blank at Jarvis. Then they turned around and walked back to their apartment, leaving him there on the beach where he was found a few hours later. Karl swore he had no prior knowledge that he suspected that's what Velda was going to do.

Laura Shackleford suffered no real damage from the "date-rape" drug she was administered. She was damn lucky, and she knows it. She continues her painting and is beginning to have real success with it. More importantly, perhaps, she's gained a new perspective on life, and how precious it is.

Me? I'm getting closer and closer to Elly, and she to me. We are definitely a couple now, and once in a great while her schedule and mine permit her to spend a bit of time at my house, alone—except for my parakeet Janey. And the good news is that her son Martin is getting almost friendly toward me.

Elly still urges me to become a romance writer instead of a crime writer, but I think she knows that'll not happen. However, I am thinking of joining that little jazz group trumpet player Jim Watson has asked me to consider. That could be fun, once again.

And Balls is talking about actually taking a vacation. He has more than a month coming to him. He says that Lorraine, his wife, wants to go to Paris, and he admits to thinking about it. Maybe Elly and I will go with them. That would be fun.

Summer is fully here now at the Outer Banks. The tourists have arrived. The weather is great, and most days I feel like all is right with the world.

CPSIA information can be obtained
at www.ICGtesting.com
Printed in the USA
LVHW041927100120
643231LV00002B/114/P